Scandalous

Edited by Zak Jane Keir

www.sincyrpublishing.com
sincyr.submissions@gmail.com

Compilation Copyright © 2021 SinCyr Publishing, University Place, WA 98466

A Few Minor Side Effects Copyright © 2021 Kristan X
Bring Me A Stranger Home Copyright © 2021 Elizabeth Coldwell
After The Show Copyright © 2021 Sprocket J. Rydyr
Master of the House Copyright © 2021 Jordan Monroe
I Confess Copyright © 2021 Eve Ray
If A Tree Falls Copyright © 2021 Louise Kane
Again Tomorrow Copyright © 2021 Elliot Sawyer
Guilt For Two Copyright © 2021 Dilo Keith
Scandaleuse Copyright © 2021 Colton Aalto
Twinkletoes © 2021 Zak Jane Keir
Fat Slut Copyright © 2021 Allison Armstrong
Patriot Copyright © 2021 Ralph Greco, Jr.

Print ISBN: 978-1-948780-31-5
Cover by Lee Moyer
Edit by Zak Jane Keir
Copy Edit by Sienna Saint-Cyr

CONTENTS

A FEW MINOR SIDE EFFECTS

Kristan X

The Xenadocin Trials were carried out over the course of two years in the early 1990s. Back then, Broad River University had a strong reputation for experimental drug development, with a number of high-profile successes. Records of the Xenadocin Trials are, however, *extremely* difficult to come by, even in the university's own archives. Urban legend has it that the researchers involved shredded much of their work when the story hit the newspapers.

The facts of the case as they are generally known are quite simple. Xenadocin was intended as a preventative therapeutic for a range of conditions, primarily heart failure. However, the drug had a number of unintended side effects – side effects which are aptly described by one participant in this personal account from a post-trial interview:

***

I didn't notice anything at all until about an hour after the first dose, at which point the effects came on rather strongly. The most overwhelming impression I had was of... well... arousal. One minute everything was normal, and the next I felt this incredible rush of desire. Suddenly it felt as though if I wasn't able to get off in the next few minutes I might just die from frustration. It really was that immediate and that urgent.

It did shock me, somewhat. I remember sitting there, sweating profusely. There was a nurse who was taking my observations – a very pretty nurse with a button nose and a streak of pink in her hair. I could smell her, and having her body that close to me, all warm and soft and feminine... it was almost too much to bear.

I did whatever I could to distract myself. I counted to a hundred, and then backwards down to zero. I imagined the most unappealing things I could to try and switch off that arousal... but it just wouldn't go. I was rock hard, and even shifting in my seat was enough to kind of... well... stimulate me.

Pretty soon it was almost out of control. I had to excuse myself and go to the men's room and... well... deal with the situation there. It didn't take long, I can tell you. As a matter of fact, I barely had to touch myself before I was done – that's how turned-on I was.

***

The above test subject got off relatively lightly, it would appear. This account comes from an early trial, where only a small dose of the drug was given. Most trials which followed used both a higher concentration and a higher dose – with results that were accordingly more dramatic.

While the few accounts of early trials that do exist make for interesting reading, it is the details of later *group* trials that are the most revelatory – at least when it comes to some of the not-so-infamous long-term properties of Xenadocin.

The vast majority of group trials took place during the summer, and usually involved six subjects apiece – most often three males and three females. For the duration of the trials, most of which lasted a week at least, participants would be sequestered together in on-campus accommodation – a setting which would be familiar to most of them, given that the vast majority of volunteers for medical testing at BRU were cash-strapped students.

The quantitative results from almost all the group trials are nothing exceptional. They read as you might expect: a dull litany of pulse, respiration, and blood pressure readings. It is in the qualitative appraisals that we find the most interesting subject matter. Here's a particularly interesting account by one female test subject from an early trial.

***

Before the trial I was, I suppose, kind of a shy girl. Unlike some people, I really didn't like talking about my love life, even to my close friends. It just made me feel… embarrassed. Awkward. Part of it was that I'd had only very limited experiences, I think. I lost my virginity quite late, and I was always very conscious of that.

When I participated in the trial, that all changed.

It was a little like a trapdoor opening inside my brain, and allowing all of my anxiety and shame and worry around that kind of thing to just drain away. I remember feeling that very distinctly, not long after the first dose was administered. And, of course, at the same time I was getting steadily more and more excited.

There were two boys at the trial who I really liked. We'd been talking – flirting, I suppose – before we all had our shots. I say flirting, but it was all very demure and they were extremely gentlemanly. They were polite and kind, and mostly it felt as though they were just looking out for me.

Well, not long after my dose I decided I'd like to cuddle up with them. And so I got up and moved to sit between them on the sofa where they were perched, and they cuddled up close to me, and it was lovely and warm and safe.

Normally I'd have been terribly anxious about even going near a boy, especially knowing that the researchers were watching our every move through the cameras. But that anxiety just wasn't there. I wanted it, and I wanted it desperately. It was like a hot glow, deep down inside of me, shining out through my skin. That glow kind of protected me.

When we started kissing that was nice, too. And it felt so natural – the most normal and natural and right thing in the world. I was kissing both of them in turn, and they were running their hands all over me, and pretty soon I was running my hands all over them. They both had hard-ons – nice, big, solid, throbbing hard-ons. Feeling them through their trousers made me want to hold them naked in my hand. And why not, I thought? Why should I be ashamed of that?

So I did it. I undid one boy's trousers and reached in and pulled his cock out. I had never dared to do that before – not once in my life – but now I did it without hesitation.

Oh, it felt incredibly good in my hand. Just right, firm and twitching and hot. It felt so good that, after stroking it for a minute, I draped myself over his lap and started sucking him. His cock filled up my mouth, and that felt good, and I kept pushing deeper, even though it made me drool and made tears come to my eyes. But it felt good, even to do that – even to make myself drool.

Without really realising it I had started kind of bucking my hips, thrusting my backside up in the air. The other boy took that as a cue, and a minute later his hands were on my hips and he was grinding against me, quite slow and gentle at first but, as I responded, he got more and more excited. Eventually he hitched up my skirt and pulled down my underwear, and eased himself into me. I was certainly wet enough by that stage!

Two boys, both at once. That was something I'd never thought I would ever do – something that girls like me simply didn't do. And yet here I was, and it was beautiful. They were so gentle with me, those boys, holding me, and whispering to me as they fucked me, about how good I felt; both of them, both rigid, twitching cocks slipping in and out of my body.

While this was happening, the other test subjects were fucking, too. I wasn't really paying attention to them; but I did notice that they were naked now, and moving together, and filling the room with little sounds of fucking – pleasant little moans and coos. There was no shyness, no shame. No hiding what we were doing from one another. The room was just full of people happily and languidly fucking away.

I don't know how to explain it other than to say that it felt right. Still does feel right. We all wanted it, then and there. And is there really anything that we should be ashamed of in that? I don't think so. And, certainly, I'm not at all ashamed of what I did. It was, I suppose, one of the most intense sexual experiences of my life so far. And normally something like that, for me at least, would have been coloured by terrific nervousness and awkwardness. But, for whatever reason, I simply didn't feel that. As a matter of fact, I still look back on that day with immense fondness.

***

The warm tones with which this participant speaks of the trial are not unusual. No amount of research can turn up an account by any test subject who had an adverse reaction, or whose experience during the trial was anything less than stunningly positive.

And here we reach the crux of the matter – the reason why the Xenadocin Trials should be more than just an embarrassing footnote in BRU's long history of drug development. The short-term effects of the drug are practically the stuff of legend – touted by newspapers worldwide… but so salacious are these stories of uncontrollable arousal that the long-term beneficial effects have rarely been examined in any detail.

***

The immediate effects faded within about 24 hours. I think I must have spent almost all that time masturbating. I lay in bed and humped the sheets and fucked myself with my fingers and bit my pillow and came over and over and over again. It was intense – maybe too intense! I was kind of relieved when I woke up the next day and the horniness had gone down a little.

But still, it wasn't gone completely. Or, if it was, the memory of being that horny for that long was still kind of a turn-on. I mean… it's kind of a turn-on thinking about it now. What a needy, slutty little animal I was for those 24 hours!

I guess that whether it was a lingering aftereffect or just a memory doesn't really matter. The point is that I couldn't stop thinking about getting laid. It was like that trip had jerked something loose inside of me, flipped a switch.

So I did something I'd always dreamed about, but never had the courage to actually do before: I went out to the campus nightclub every night for a week and took home a different boy each time.

Doing something really excessive and slutty like that had always been a fantasy of mine. I wanted to splurge. Really overindulge. God it felt good. Messy and exhausting, but powerful, too. That week might just have been one of the best weeks of my life – and I'm sure I owe it all to the drug trial. Were it not for that, I don't think I'd ever have had the courage (or maybe, I should say, the need) to follow through on my fantasy.

And the sex... that was wild, too. I did things I'd never done with any boy before. Pornstar things. I went on top, and fucked a boy until he was just about to come and then went down on him, whipped the condom off and swallowed his load. Eye contact all the while. His cock was still hot from being inside of me. God – I'm shivering now just thinking about it.

I'd say that being in the trial really did me a lot of good. It gave me the impetus to try things I'd always wanted to try. It put me way more in control of my sex life. And I don't know whether that's, strictly speaking, an effect of the drug, or more a result of what happened after... but I don't think it matters either way. All that matters is that it was a formative experience, and I wouldn't change a thing.

***

From these accounts it is, perhaps, possible to see why the details of the Xenadocin trials piqued the interest of the tabloid press. Many of the accounts that are still available are rich with lurid details, and almost all share common themes: the drug prompted not just a 24-hour period of uncontrollable arousal, but a wider sexual awakening. It enabled participants to pursue sexual fantasies, to experiment without fear, and to talk about their experiences without shame.

While the day-long period of arousal appears to be limited in its effects, the wider changes are not. The freeing effects of the drug appear to last for as long as any follow-up records persist – even though no physical trace of Xenadocin remains in the body.

***

The first time I ever sucked another guy's dick was during the trial. He was a participant too, and we'd been eyeing each other up pretty steadily for the last few hours. It was getting towards the end of the first day and nothing crazy had happened yet – almost to the point I was sure if we'd been given a placebo or something.

This guy was a proper jock. Rugby player. Broad-shouldered. Obviously worked out. Kind of tough and surly. First time I made eye contact with him, he proper sneered at me. And I sneered right back. Figured he was just an arsehole, nothing more than that.

But then a couple of hours passed with all of us participants hanging out in the kitchen, drinking endless cups of tea and making small talk and nervously joking about some of the rumours we'd heard about; the kind of thing that happened at these trials. And as the hours passed, I got this feeling. I can't explain it. It was like... even though he seemed like a wanker, I couldn't stop looking at him.

It really puzzled me at first. Because when I looked at him, the warm, excited feeling in my chest would kind of jump. Which didn't make sense. Because I was straight, and really, I ought to get that looking at the girls, if anyone. But no. It was this guy I couldn't keep my eyes off of, and when we made eye contact again, I swear my heart started racing right then and there.

I'd never really told anyone, but I'd always been kind of curious about certain things. Like, I'd think about it when I jacked off. About, for example, what it would be like to go down on another guy. It wasn't a big thing, really, just something that I'd think about sometimes, kind of idly. Sometimes when I was jacking off, I'd get these little moments where I'd imagine a cock in my mouth, or being on my knees, or something like that.

Well, now it wasn't just little flashes. Now I felt like I could hardly think of anything else. This guy – this rugby player jock wanker – I wanted to suck his dick. I wanted that very badly. So badly my heart was hammering and I felt kind of light-headed and my hands felt shaky and tingly.

I looked at him. Stared at him. Like I was trying to transmit that idea by telepathy to him. After a minute, it seemed almost like it worked, because he looked back at me, scowled for a moment, and then – very, very slightly – jerked his head towards the door.

I have never been that excited before in my life. I hopped to my feet, made an excuse, and went back to my room. The guy was there a minute later. We hardly spoke. We both knew what we wanted. I let him in and shut the door and for a moment we just glared at each other. And then I went down on my knees, and he reached into his pants, and I saw that he was hard already, real hard, and big, and he got himself out with this rough little twitch. His cock was just there, in my face, and maybe I hesitated for a moment, like waiting for permission, because he jerked it towards me.

"Go on," he said. And that was all I needed. I rocked forward and wrapped my lips around him and started sucking. I'd never done that before, but right away it just felt right. Totally normal. Really incredibly good, having my mouth filled. And the way he grunted. Every time I pushed forward to try and take him a little bit deeper, I felt my own dick throbbing in response.

I had my hands on his thighs, gripping fistfuls of his pants. I wasn't worried about choking. Actually, I was pulling on him, trying to pull him into me. All I could think about was that I wanted my mouth to be completely full. Full of him. And I wanted to make him come with my mouth, even though I'd never done this before, and I didn't know if I was any good – I *really* wanted to make him come.

And I did, actually. I'm proud of how quickly I managed it. And of how, when he did, I kept his dick in my mouth while it twitched and pulsed and I swallowed every last bit of his come. I swear, I actually had a kind of orgasm myself while that was happening – this full-body pulse of warmth and tingling that ran right through me, head to toe.

As first times go, it was a pretty good one. At the time, I chalked it up to the drug – everyone said it made you lose your inhibitions for a while. Made you go kind of crazy. But I didn't realise then that it would actually last. That this wouldn't be a one-off. That this was actually going to pretty much change my life.

**

The potential of a drug that can do so much, so permanently, from just a single dose is almost limitless. So what lead to the demise of the two-year development program? What destroyed Xenadocin before it could ever reach the market?

By the late-stage trials, the researchers were certainly aware of the side effects of the drug, and had indeed begun to pivot from developing a therapeutic preventative to a sexual enhancer. After all, the results it produced beat anything that existed on the market at the time, and the drug was universally positively received by trial participants. By bringing such a drug to market, they stood to make millions.

The only fly in the ointment was the university. Broad River had a prestigious reputation when it came to drug development, and the consensus was that the authorities would never risk tarnishing their image by being the institution responsible for creating a new strain of superviagra.

These fears proved to be well-founded. In December of 1998, a student who had been involved in a trial sold their story to a tabloid newspaper. Within days, reporters had descended on campus, and lurid tales of what had gone on during the trials were making headlines around the globe.

Of course, funding was immediately pulled from the project. No further trials were completed, and the drug – promising as it was – was left to languish in the archives forevermore, a smutty stain on BRU's otherwise-spotless reputation.

These days, the story of the Xenadocin Trials is little more than an urban legend – a bit of trivia which sometimes crops up in a sidebar of the student paper, or is slyly referenced in the Union pub quizzes. Most students, when polled, are aware that BRU was in some way involved in almost patenting an orgy drug... but their familiarity with the story goes no further.

The Trials, however, were both real and incredible. Xenadocin was not just an aphrodisiac, but a powerful agent for long-term change: a drug which eradicated shame. In a world where shame is more powerful a weapon than ever, is it not perhaps time for a follow-up to BRU's most infamous study?

BRING ME A STRANGER HOME

Elizabeth Coldwell

The next person who walked through the door would be allowed to use her body in any way they wished. She sat, listening patiently for the sound of her husband's tread on the stairs, her wrists constrained by the silk scarves which bound her to the chair, wondering who he would bring home with him this time.

It was a ritual they had been acting out on the final Friday of every month for more than a year now, a ritual in which she had been a willing and eager participant from the start.

Sitting here in the silky white panties, lace-topped stockings, and high heels which was all he allowed her to wear, Lisa relished her feelings of vulnerability and strange excitement. Once a month, her relief came at the hands of someone unknown, recruited by her husband and brought back here on the spur of the moment.

How many had there been? Keeping count was one way of passing the time until Aidan returned. The first one she would always remember. Jim, eighteen years old and a sixth-former at the boys' public school down the road, his eyes widening at the sight of Lisa tied to her chair, dressed in the trashiest of lingerie, with a gag in her mouth. No doubt Aidan had explained something of the set-up as they made their way back to the Hall in his vintage Rolls Royce, but it was one thing to be told you were about to have free rein with a stranger's wife, and quite another to walk into a room and see her waiting for you, half-naked and helpless.

When the lad finally realised this was no joke, and Lisa really had been trussed up for his benefit, his reaction was that of a small child let loose in a toy shop. He came to kneel in front of her; close up, she could see how young he was, his skin smooth and flushed with excitement, his limbs coltish. His black hair fell untidily into his eyes and he smelled of lemony soap.

His hands reached for her breasts, barely constrained by a sheer black nylon half-cup bra. Her nipples peeped over the top of the cups, roused into hardness by his touch. She wore a matching pair of crotchless panties and had been tied so her legs were widely splayed, revealing her pussy lips through the split in the cheap knickers.

Jim's wandering hands moved down to her pussy and explored the soft, wet folds of flesh. He stroked her clit with infuriating lightness, and she moaned her frustration from behind her gag. Taking pity on her, he removed the strip of sodden cloth from her mouth. Eyes imploring him, she murmured, "Harder, please…"

"Lisa, what have I told you?" Aidan snapped. "You know you're not allowed to speak." He turned and addressed the boy. "She's broken one of the rules. Remember what I told you on the way here, Jim? If she breaks the rules, she has to be punished."

"You said she likes to be spanked," Jim replied.

"That's right. And you'd like to spank her, wouldn't you?"

Jim's eyes widened. "I..."

"Of course, you would," Aidan said.

"Yes, I would," Jim finally answered.

Aidan reached for the ties binding Lisa to the chair. He unfastened them quickly and lifted her to her feet. "Sit down," he urged Jim. Looking slightly dazed, Jim did as he was told.

Aidan helped him to guide Lisa into place over his long legs, clad in neatly pressed grey trousers. Their thin material could not conceal the stiffness of his erection, pressing up eagerly against her stomach. He'd probably been hard since the moment he walked into the room.

"Lisa, you know this spanking is your choice, don't you?" Aidan always asked her this, and she always said yes. *Show our guest you consent. Even if they think they're in charge here, we know the truth, don't we?*

"Yes, sir."

For a moment, nothing further happened. Lisa wondered whether Jim was looking to Aidan for more instructions, but with her head bowed to the floor she couldn't see what was taking place.

Then, without warning, she felt a sharp slap on her buttock, quickly followed by a second. If Aidan was coaching Jim in what she responded to, he was doing a good job. Fast, rhythmic spanks were by far the most effective way to punish her, piling pain upon pain without giving her the chance to recover. She writhed and kicked on the boy's lap, knowing with every movement she was not only stimulating his cock but also giving Aidan a perfect view of her swelling pussy through the open crotch of her panties.

Jim continued to pepper her backside with slaps, occasionally catching the tender skin at the tops of her thighs as she tried to wriggle away from his relentless palm. She cast mute glances at Aidan through tear-filled eyes, wanting him to bring an end to this treatment, and yet aware that pain was now being replaced with a different sensation, a deep undercurrent of pleasure. She tried to press herself harder against Jim's thick erection, wanting to rub herself against him, but it was all too much for him. With a groan, he slumped back in the chair, and she realised that he had come in his trousers.

She hoped Aidan would order her to lick him back to hardness, so he could give her the fucking she craved, but, to her intense disappointment, Jim asked to leave. "My study period will be over," he explained. "I've got to get back to school before I'm missed, or I'll be the one who gets punished."

Aidan was careful who he chose to bring back, thinking not only of Lisa's personal safety, but also of the scandal that would arise if their games became common knowledge in the village. Their neighbours viewed Aidan, who'd made his money managing rock stars, with suspicion. The parties he and Lisa occasionally threw for their musician friends were already regarded as one step away from Satanic ritual;

it made no sense to give the gossips a concrete foundation for their slanders and innuendoes.

When she quizzed Aidan later, he claimed to have found Jim skulking in the school grounds, smoking an illicit cigarette when he should have been working on his Latin prep.

Aidan's preferred hunting ground became the Magpie Inn, on the outskirts of the village, where he would recruit some businessman who was staying there overnight. At other times, he would drive into a neighbouring hamlet to see who he could bring back. He had threatened Lisa repeatedly that one day he would travel all the way to Southampton, the nearest big centre of population, in search of a suitable playmate. She knew he would never leave her unattended for so long, even though the bindings were loose enough she could free herself if she really needed to and her smartphone was close by, but it thrilled her to think that one day he just might carry out his threat and trawl the city's streets on her behalf.

The afternoon that burned most deeply in her memory, however, was the one when Aidan returned with two men, both builders, who he had discovered working on renovations to the local railway station. They looked rough and ready, dirt ground into their skin and under their fingernails, their eyes hard in their sunburnt faces. It had been a hot, humid July day, and neither man wore more than a pair of cut-off denim shorts and steel-toed work boots, spattered with dried mud and cement. As she looked at the pair warily, the thought of them working on her body in tandem triggered a spasm of fear and expectancy low in her belly.

"She's all yours," Aidan said, standing back to watch the proceedings. He didn't use their names, and that turned Lisa on even more. *Even if they think they're in charge here, we know the truth, don't we?*

On this occasion, she wore a scarlet-and-black basque designed to thrust her breasts upward irresistibly, and the tiniest black G-string, the nylon fabric sheer enough to reveal the dark shadow of her pubic hair.

As always, there was a momentary hesitation while they gauged whether this was a set-up. Then, realising they were being given absolute permission to do whatever they wished to the luscious woman who was bound and waiting in front of them, they began to take advantage of Aidan's generous offer.

Their first act was to free her from the chair. The taller of the two, who had short, peroxide-blond hair and a taut, muscular body, untied her and hauled her to her feet. He thrust his hand without ceremony between her legs to get a good feel of her already lubricated pussy through her G-string. His companion, shorter, stockier and with dark hair shaved almost to his scalp to disguise the fact of how quickly it was receding, turned his attention to her breasts. He pulled them from the cups of the basque and mauled them with his grimy hands. He pinched her nipples between his thumbs and index fingers, causing her to moan. Though his touch was rough and unsophisticated, there was much more of pleasure than pain in her response.

His blond companion yanked her G-string halfway down her thighs and shoved two fingers up into her wetness. He chuckled when he pulled those fingers back out, coated with her cream. "You're right, the slut is really up for this." He still sounded as though he couldn't quite believe this was happening. "She'll do anything, right?"

Aidan nodded. It wasn't entirely true: Lisa had her hard limits, and a word at her disposal to unleash should anyone breach those boundaries. So far, she'd never had to use it.

"Okay, then, get down on your knees."

She obeyed immediately, watching as he popped open the button fly of his shorts. He hadn't bothered with any underwear, and she was treated to the sight of his cock springing from its thatch of dark hair. Already half-hard, it was conspicuously bigger than average, and she shuddered with guilty pleasure at the thought of taking something that size in front of Aidan.

The other man followed his lead. Though he couldn't match his friend in terms of length, what he had was thick and enticing, and she yearned to touch it.

"Suck me," the blond ordered, pressing his cockhead to her lips. She opened her mouth and took the fat head inside. He tasted sweaty from his labours, but his uniquely male aroma had its own power to arouse her, and she licked him eagerly. As she did, she couldn't help but be aware of Aidan standing to one side, watching everything that happened with cool detachment. Whatever was asked of her, she would do it for his pleasure as well as hers, like she always did.

"D'you want some of this?" the blond asked his friend, as casually as if he'd been sharing a lunchtime butty. With a grunt of assent, the dark-haired man came to join him, and now a second cock was thrust towards her lips, in search of the same treatment. Eyes downcast submissively, Lisa accepted its arrival without complaint, slurping her tongue over first one fleshy crown, then the next.

Urged on by the two men, she sucked each of them in turn, taking as much hot cock-flesh into her mouth as she could. Though she tried to set the pace, their eagerness, their delight at being enveloped in the wet vacuum of her throat overtook them. Soon, they were both as good as fucking her face, the blond's hand gripping Lisa's hair as he thrust at her with short, stabbing strokes.

She couldn't believe Aidan remained as calm as he did, watching her being taken so forcefully. He didn't even stroke himself through his jeans, even though she could see from the corner of her eye the thick outline of his dick through the tight, faded denim. Only when these two had left would he satisfy his own desires, burying his erection deep in her body. For now, he remained content to watch and wait.

She was drawn back to the moment when the dark-haired guy wrenched his cock from her throat's grip. It came loose with a popping sound, and as she turned away, she saw traces of her bubblegum-pink lipstick smeared along its length.

"We can fuck her, yeah?" The question was directed at Aidan.

"I've told you," Aidan replied. "You can do what you want."

"You freak me out, you know that, mate," the blond said. "You're seriously going to let us fuck your missus? Anyone tried that with my bird, I'd hunt him down and put him in the hospital."

"We have an arrangement," Aidan told him. "Everything we have, we share, and that includes each other. If you can't cope with it, you can always leave now."

"What, and not get to use that juicy cunt of hers? No way."

To be referred to so crudely and yet desired so much caused Lisa to tremble. She wanted to feel his huge cock thrusting into her, driving the breath from her. She suspected, as far as he was concerned, getting off was all that mattered, with little thought for his partner's pleasure. The thought of being treated as barely more than a sex doll excited her intensely.

"You want her cunt?" the dark-haired man asked his friend, still acting as though Lisa wasn't really in the room. "Well, we've both had her mouth, so I guess that leaves me her arse, doesn't it?" The prospect sounded, to Lisa's ears, like the most thrilling he'd ever considered.

As for Lisa, this was the only one of her fantasies that had remained unfulfilled. She'd been made to do so many gorgeously depraved things, both by Aidan and the strangers he'd brought home with him, but she'd never taken a cock in both pussy and arse at the same time.

She remained kneeling while Aidan tossed the two builders a condom each and watched them sheathe their cocks. No one could fuck her without one. The men conversed in low tones, obviously discussing how best they were going to manoeuvre her between them. At last the blond lay on the floor on his back, dick sticking up, rigid as a tree trunk. His companion guided an unresisting Lisa into position, encouraging her to sink on to his massive length. The dimensions of him took her breath away, parting her walls wide as gravity dragged her down. A good third of him still remained outside her when he eventually bottomed out in her wet velvet vault.

She'd barely had time to adjust to the feel of this monster when she sensed his friend stroking the entrance to her arse with a curious finger. The pressure grew harder, until it slid inside, guided by the juices that had trickled down from her pussy to soak the length of her cleft. It felt good, but she knew it would be even better when his finger was replaced with his shaft.

"You love this, don't you?' he commented. "Your husband's right. You're a filthy little slut who'll do anything for cock."

The words should have stung, but she knew he was right. Doing whatever she was told, letting strangers use her for their own gratification; since she'd been with Aidan, he'd helped her open up the part of herself that revelled in such forbidden urges, learning what it meant to obey. Truly scandalous behaviour, but so satisfying, so…necessary. She almost pitied the women who craved to be guided in the ways of submission and had yet to meet the person who would lead them along that path.

"Do it," she found herself murmuring. "Fuck me. Take my arse."

The man needed no second invitation. She was aware of a brief, stinging discomfort as her ring tried to fight against the intrusion, then she relaxed and he was inside her, stretching her tight back-hole as widely as his friend was stretching her in front.

The two thrust hard and deep, taking a moment to establish a rhythm, but once they found it, they moved in rapid synchrony. She'd been fucked with much more finesse, but never with such brute, basic need. She reached down between her own body and the blond's, seeking her clit where it nestled at the apex of her slit, and stroking it in swift, teasing circles that couldn't fail to bring her to orgasm.

To her surprise, the blond came first; she might have expected the clutching pressure of her arse to hasten his friend's orgasm instead. The feel of him coming inside her had been enough to spark her own climax, her muscles spasming around the softening cock in her pussy and the still solid one in her arse. His friend followed quickly, unable to resist the pressure of Lisa's clenching passage. At last, they collapsed in a sweating tangle on the floor, their softening dicks sliding from her body.

In moments, the two men had dressed and were ready to leave. Would she be the talk of the building site tomorrow? Lisa guessed not. Aidan seemed to have the knack of making sure the people he brought here never revealed the secrets of the game they played.

The blond turned at the door of the playroom as Aidan had prepared to take the two men back to their work detail, and winked at Lisa. "If you want more of the same, you know where to find me."

As she sat reliving the experience, she found herself hoping Aidan had managed to track the two builders down again. It was a forlorn hope, she knew: not only would the work on the station be long finished by now, but it was an unspoken rule between them that he never brought the same person to the house twice.

The door swung open, startling her. Aidan stood in the doorway, and behind him was a woman in her mid-twenties, with dark-blonde hair falling in soft waves to her shoulders and a slender figure. She was dressed as though for an interview, in a floral cotton dress with a black jacket over the top, and she seemed distinctly shocked by the sight of Lisa's full, bare breasts and submissive posture.

It would not be the first time Aidan had watched her being pleasured by another woman. The first time it happened, he kept Lisa oblivious to the fact, the scarf he had wrapped around her head before he had left acting as an effective blindfold. Lisa had been aware that the hands stroking her body were soft and delicate, but she had thought, perhaps, her husband had been recruiting among the sixth formers once more. The fingers and mouth that worked on her had given her no clue to their owner's identity, and only when Aidan had removed her blindfold did she realise she had been brought to orgasm by a middle-aged woman with scraped-back hair and horn-rimmed glasses.

Already visualising in her head how this encounter was to go, Lisa was to receive a shock of her own, for unlike every other month, her husband did not encourage the newcomer to approach the chair. Instead, he came over to her himself and reached for the scarves that bound her wrists to the chair.

"It's been a long time since you've tasted the crop," Aidan murmured as he hauled her to her feet.

"Have I been extra-bad this month, sir?" Lisa asked, her lips quirking in a grin.

Aidan turned to the blonde, who stared open-mouthed at what was happening before her. "If you look in the cabinet at the side of the bed to your left, you'll find a riding crop. Could you fetch it for me while I ask my wife to assume the punishment position?"

The woman looked as though she was about to refuse, but instead, she opened the cabinet Aidan had indicated and retrieved the crop. Gingerly, as though it might bite her, she handed it to him.

"Thank you. Six strokes, I think, Lisa." He ran his hands over her buttocks, which were left bare by the thong back of her panties. "You know the drill. Tell me you want this."

"Yes, sir. I want this. I *need* this." She meant every word.

"Very good. Count them and thank me. Any mistakes, and we go back to one. Do you understand?"

"Yes, sir." Lisa clutched the chair back, her bottom thrust outward, awaiting the first blow. Aidan did not keep her waiting long; the crop tapped her left cheek, lightly, as Aidan measured his stance. Then she sensed, rather than saw him raise his arm. The crop whistled briefly through the air and landed squarely across her buttocks, leaving a line of fire in its wake. "One, thank you," she whispered.

The second and third blows followed swiftly, parallel to the first. Again, she thanked Aidan even as the pain coursed through her. His fingers gently traced the weals the crop had raised on her skin. "Her bottom marks so beautifully, don't you think?" he asked the blonde.

"I...I suppose so," she replied.

"Come here and have a good look," he urged. The woman stepped close; Aidan caught hold of her hand and encouraged her to stroke the crop marks. Her touch was light and tentative; despite herself, Lisa could not help wishing Aidan would coax her into running her fingers down into the crease between her legs, to discover how wet and excited she was.

She was disappointed when Aidan ordered the blonde to step back and raised the crop again. The final three strokes were dispatched in quick succession, each one moving lower until the vicious instrument whipped the soft flesh at the top of Lisa's thighs. The pain was excruciating, even to someone who had been punished as often as Lisa had, and she could not prevent herself from sobbing as she thanked Aidan for the last of the six.

"Very good, my darling, very good," he murmured, his fingers once more soothing her injured bottom before dipping into the well of her sex and beginning to rub at her clit. Fresh pleasure zinged through Lisa's already overstimulated body, and when he slipped a finger into her channel, doubling the sensation, she convulsed in orgasm around the probing digit.

"So, what do you think, Hayley?" Aiden asked their guest, his fingers still playing wicked games in Lisa's pussy as the final aftershocks of her climax faded away.

"Well, I'll admit your approach is a little unorthodox," she replied, "but I think I'm going to enjoy being your housekeeper very much."

With a wink to Lisa that told her how much he'd admired her fortitude as she took her cropping, Aidan ushered Hayley out of the room. Lisa could hardly keep the smile from her face. Yet again, her husband had reminded her quite why she loved him so much. After all, who else would think to turn a routine interview for their newest member of staff into such a deliciously punishing experience?

AFTER THE SHOW

Sprocket J. Rydyr

Bass thumps through the venue: the music that plays between sets to keep the crowd pumped. Your body is still thrumming with adrenaline, vibrating like a tuning fork, long after the end of your set. Your band's never had such a good show before, and for the first time in the five years Bone Titty's been together, you think that maybe this isn't just a pipe dream, after all. Maybe you really *are* going to be a rockstar.

Your act's too niche to get a real following, or at least that's what everyone tells you. Five small-town enby queers, none of you white, playing a weird mixture of old-school queercore and thrash metal in whatever dive bars are willing to take a chance on you. Which means you're mostly playing gigs where you and your crew are screaming about what racist, transmisogynistic queer-bashers have done to fuck up your lives, right into the faces of the those same racist, transmisogynistic queer-bashers. Most nights, if you get crickets during your set and scattered, baffled applause when you finish, it's a triumph. More often, you get beer spat on you, and maybe a bloodied nose by the end of the night.

But tonight… You've never had an audience like this before. This wild, this *into* it. Not a big crowd, in the grand scheme of things—probably less than fifty people—but fucking *raucous*. You couldn't see clearly through the stage lights, but the pit looked like total chaos. You're pretty sure you heard some property damage. More importantly, you heard *singing*. Not just on your cover of *I Wanna Be Sedated*, not just on the chorus of that song Atul wrote that's the closest thing to a hit your band has: on damn near every single song. When you started playing the one you wrote for the new album that only dropped last month, the song that took you half a year to get right because it's so fucking personal, and the crowd lit up like a house on fire and started howling right along with you… *Fuck*.

Best feeling in the world.

You're still riding that high even as the next band starts setting up. You're not drunk, but you stumble into the bathroom like you are. You've got the most idiotic grin on your face when you look in the dingy mirror over the sink. It should probably be embarrassing, but it isn't. You've earned every inch of that smile.

This venue's as much of a dump as every other place your band has ever played. No green room, barely even a stage, and the bathroom reeks of piss, beer, and puke. If you ever do move up in the world, you'll miss playing in places like this. There's something about these squalid hellholes that feels like home to you. It feels like pouring out your heart and soul onstage with your bandmates, whether anybody shows up to your gig or not. Like sleeping on a moving bus that smells like five people who haven't showered in a week. You can't imagine any other life.

The bathroom door opens as you're washing your hands. You don't pay it any mind, until your eyes happen to catch on the mirror and see a familiar reflection smirking back at you from between the myriad band stickers covering its dirty surface. You turn around to face Ari, who's got their back against the tiled wall and their arms folded over their chest in a way that makes their well-formed arm muscles stand out in startling definition. They've got a sly, dangerous look on their face you've seen too many times by now to not know exactly what it means.

You and Ari have been hooking up off and on for the better part of a year now, starting just a few weeks after they replaced Xaime on drums. If your bandmates have noticed—and how could they not have, at this point?—then nobody's had the nerve to bring it up. It's not like you're in love, or even dating or anything. Just the two of you blowing off some steam together from time to time because a) neither of you has the time or inclination for a relationship and b) both of you tend to get all keyed up after shows. Plus, Ari's hot as hell.

"Sick show tonight," Ari says when they know they've got your attention. "You were on fire."

You wipe your hands—still shaking from the excess energy coursing through your body and now from anticipation as well—on your shredded jeans. The sound of your pulse in your ears is suddenly louder than the bass seeping through the thin bathroom walls. "That your way of saying I looked hot?"

Ari smirks at you. "That your way of fishing for compliments?" Ari's fucking gorgeous. Their wavy black hair is still rumpled and sweaty from forty minutes behind a drum kit. The veins on their forearms and the backs of their hands are still standing out from the exertion of their performance and you want to run your tongue along every single one of them. Their beautiful brown eyes are hidden behind those ludicrous aviator shades they wear onstage—they've been photosensitive ever since a concussion they got years before you met and stage lights play hell with it—but you can still see they're ablaze with impatient excitement.

Normally, you wait until you're back at the bus or whatever shitty hotel you're booked into for the night. Normally, you wait until the others are all crashed out asleep. But, judging from the familiar quirk of Ari's lips, the angle of their eyebrows as they size you up from behind their aviators, they don't want to wait. And maybe, on a normal night, you'd have too much dignity to fuck Ari in a public restroom, but tonight you're high on success and you feel just as reckless as they do.

They've got the small of your back pressed up against the cold lip of the sink before you can even give voice to your desires, and you find yourself chuckling against their eager lips. They kiss you rough and sloppy—all urgency and no finesse—and you kiss them back the same way. You're making out in a venue bathroom; finesse would be grossly out of place.

You twine your fingers in their sweaty hair and they grunt and grip your thighs just below your ass, hefting you up until you're sitting on the filthy restroom sink.

You're going to need three showers just to feel clean again after this, but you're beyond caring about that right now. You wrap your legs around their hips and kiss them so deeply you both nearly choke.

Ari's tongue tastes like beer and cigarettes and the cinnamon gum they use to try to smother the other flavors. When they slip their tongue free from your mouth and run it down the length of your throat, it feels like liquid fire. You're already sweating more than you were onstage; you struggle out of your denim vest and let it fall to the floor, band pins clattering on the wet tiles. Ari bites your neck and you whimper. They chuckle, smug as hell. You squeeze their ass in retaliation. "Cocky fucker," you mutter before you gently bite their ear.

Ari shivers. "You know it." They lean their hips into your body, and you can feel a hard bulge digging into you.

You burst out laughing. "You cheeky bastard! You seriously packed hard *onstage*?!"

"Fuck yeah," Ari says, without an ounce of shame. "I know how you get after a show. And I had a good feeling about this one."

"It was really something else, wasn't it?"

Ari nods and leans against you with alarming tenderness, forehead pressing to your shoulder. Their sunglasses tumble off and land on your vest. "It really was."

If you let things get too serious you're never going to be able to go through with this here, and your body is begging for you to keep going. You tug their head back by their hair and rake your teeth up the length of their neck, and they sigh.

A calloused hand slides up under the back of your shirt, fingertips tingling over bare skin on your lower back, dull pressure over your binder. They bite your shoulder through your shirt and you moan. You slip your hands down the back of their jeans, gripping them through their sweat-damp boxer briefs. They grind against you, hard packer a solid pressure even through the layers of fabric between you. You can feel yourself getting wet. Ari pushes up the fabric of your shirt and teases your lower stomach before reaching down and giving your soft packer a firm squeeze through your shorts. "How about it?" they ask, their voice a low rumble tickling your ear. They trace a finger up your zipper and circle your button.

As much as part of you wants to get fucked senseless on top of the sink, the more rational part of your mind urges you to at least relocate to a semi-private area before you two get interrupted. You heave yourself off the sink and push Ari backward toward the stalls. They follow your direction with a confident smirk. You shut the door behind you and just manage to fumble the slide lock home (thank god you managed to stumble into a stall with a working lock) before they return to sucking hickies into your neck, pushing your back against the door.

This is going to be a hard one to keep secret from your bandmates, with the way Ari's carving signatures into your flesh with their teeth. "You were so fucking good onstage tonight," Ari whispers into the delicate skin of your throat before they chase their words with their tongue. "I wanted to take you apart right then and there."

You fumble the button of your shorts open, hoping they'll take the hint; they need no further instruction, unzipping your fly with a swift jerk of their hand that doesn't quite do the trick. They fight it down the rest of the way as you lift your hips off the door to help. "You were eye-fucking me the whole set, huh?"

You can feel their grin: the press of their perfect, crooked teeth against sensitive skin. "I did have a *spectacular* view of your ass," they admit, teasing a finger along the waistband of your briefs. "Could you feel me?"

"If I could, I don't think I could've played a note." You chase their touch with your hips, though they keep their fingers tantalizingly out of reach. "Wouldn't mind feeling you right now, though."

"Oh, well, in *that* case." They slip their hand into the pocket of your briefs and wrap their fingers around your soft packer. You gasp as it presses up against your overheated flesh. They sigh, breath tickling your ear in a way that makes you shiver.

The friction of Ari rubbing and squeezing your packer through the thin back layer of your briefs probably shouldn't be enough to get you off, but you know as soon as they start that it's going to be. "What did you want to do to me?" you ask breathlessly, shifting into their touch.

"Onstage?" They smile dirtily when you nod, pausing to give your ear a playful nip before answering. "I wanted to jump right over my drum kit and take you hard under the stage lights. Right there in front of everybody."

Your whole body twitches. You close your eyes and you picture it as clear as day.

"I wanted to rub your bass between your legs until you came. I wanted to pin you to the stage and strip your clothes off with my teeth."

You whimper and grind into their touch. They pick up their pace obligingly.

"That turns you on, huh? The thought of me making you my bitch onstage?"

"*Hnnnghh,*" is the only reply you can muster.

"Such a fuckin' perv," they chuckle, cupping your balls. They bend to your collar, taking your shirt between their teeth and tugging sharply. Their packer rubs against your thigh, and you let out an embarrassing whine.

"L-little rougher," you pant, and they laugh again — a warm puff of breath against your collarbone that makes you quiver.

"Mmm, that's exactly what you'd say, draped over my drums. Panting and moaning while everybody stares…" Their hand picks up its pace, working your packer against your aching clit so vigorously your eyes cross behind closed lids. "The whole band," they continue relentlessly. "The whole audience. Bet *that'd* pack a venue: you getting fucked over my drum kit. Bend you over the riding toms, pull down your pants, spank you senseless with my drum sticks…"

You make a high keening sound and come so hard you see stars. Your legs turn to jelly; the only thing keeping you even partly upright is Ari pressing up against you, their body keeping you in place against the stall door.

They slow down but don't stop, letting you recover but not cool down. "Want more?" they ask, and you nod greedily. They speed up again, rubbing themself

41

against your thigh, and for a few seconds it's too much stimulation. As they resume whispering obscene fantasies in your ear, it swiftly moves from too much to not enough.

"Faster," you moan. "*Harder.*"

"My arms are gonna fuckin' fall off!" they tease, but they oblige. "I just played a whole set, you thirsty slut."

You wrap your arms around Ari's shoulders and sag against their body as you shudder and shake. You're moaning way too loudly for discretion, but you're too far gone to care. You're so close to a second release that you can taste it.

"Hmm, you know, I don't think I've ever spanked someone with a drum stick before," they muse. "Bet you'd be into that shit, wouldn't you?"

Ari taking you ruthlessly onstage. Disciplining you in front of an audience. If they ever did it in reality, you'd probably die of embarrassment. But thinking about it while Ari furiously jerks you off? "*Fuuuuhhhhckkk...* mmmmmmnnn..." Your legs give out completely when you come a second time, and Ari straight-up giggles with delight.

"Dude, you are *ridiculous* tonight." They press a kiss against your ear. "Don't get me wrong, I'm super into it." They glance down at the floor as they hold you steady. "Hey, uh... Any chance you don't mind getting your knees dirty?"

Well, hell. It's not like you aren't going to have to shower when you get back to the hotel anyway. Might as well go all in. You loosen your grip on Ari's shoulders and drop down to your knees by way of an answer.

Oh, this was a terrible idea. You flinch in disgust at the feeling of damp bathroom tiles, that probably haven't been cleaned in days, against the bare skin of your knees. You get to work on Ari's zipper before your sense of self-preservation can kick in.

"Here, hang on…" Ari digs a condom out of their pocket as you liberate their silicon shaft from their boxer briefs. Chances of you coming into contact with any risky bodily fluids by sucking their hard packer are pretty low, but you appreciate the gesture anyway; the packer's been down their pants all night, and it's definitely picked up some lint and sweat. They hold the packer stable while you ease the condom over it. You wrap your fingers around their shaft and make sure to make eye contact with Ari as you lean in and take their tip in your mouth because you know how much they like to watch. The taste is pretty blah—you haven't had any luck finding latex-free condoms that don't taste like boredom—but the look on their face is worth it.

They release a sigh mixed with laughter and run their fingers through your hair. "This has *got* to be the worst place we've ever fooled around."

You beg to differ. There was that sketchy motel where you were pretty sure you were going to get axe-murdered while you two boned by the ice machine, not to mention that one back alley where rats were definitely fucking even more energetically than you were, but your mouth is otherwise occupied so you don't rebut.

You take Ari's cock deeper into your mouth, not breaking contact with their eyes. You grasp near the base and give Ari a little extra pressure to grind against. They grip their fingers in your hair, staring back into your eyes. "Yeah, suck that cock," they murmur affectionately, trailing fingers over the shell of your ear. So you do.

Your knees ache and your jaw is already tired—you only sing backup but tonight was still way more singing and talking than you have to do most nights—but you absolutely fucking *devour* them anyway. You take them in until you're almost choking, eyes watering and clenching shut.

You can feel them trying to restrain themself, careful not to fuck your face too hard. You appreciate the sentiment, but you *want* to make them lose control. You keep up the pressure on the base of their cock, rubbing and pressing to produce hot friction as you bob your head vigorously.

"Ah, fuck," they sigh, hips twitching.

You pull off with a loud, sucking pop and beam up at them. You run your tongue up and down their length in messy strokes, tease the tip of your tongue around their glans, lavish attention over every exposed inch. Each time they tip their head back with a soft curse of pleasure, they make sure to bring themself back and open their eyes again so you can stare back at them. They want to see everything, and you want them to see how much you love it.

You take them up to their hilt again and they can't suppress a hard snap of their hips that drives the tip of their cock into the back of your throat. You swallow against the wave of saliva that rises up in response, fighting your gag reflex.

"Doin' okay, babe?" they pant.

In response, you start bobbing your head again, taking their length over and over as you rub the base of the packer firmly against them. It takes a few seconds for you to register the sound of the bathroom door opening, the music outside getting louder before muffling again. Ari is panting steadily now, making small, helpless thrusts into your mouth. Footsteps pass your stall without pausing. It sounds like they're staggering a bit; maybe they're too drunk to notice you're on your knees. Or maybe they think you're just throwing up.

Ari holds your gaze and tilts their head in the direction of the interloper, a silent question whether you want to stop. You shrug and keep sucking. You two have gotten it on in less private places and anyway the stranger seems more interested in using the urinals than in peeking into stalls.

Ari only just manages to stifle a moan as you grind the packer hard against them and run your tongue along their length, swirling it around the ridge of the glans. Your other hand slips between your own legs as you work Ari harder, reaching into your still-undone fly and diving beneath your briefs to trace hot circles into wet flesh. *"Mmmnffh."*

"You're so fucking hot," Ari whispers beneath their breath, chuckling soft and amazed. Their fingers curl around the base of your skull, following the vigorous motions of your head as you eagerly suck them off. The way you're slurping is way too loud for a public space, but it's impossible to be silent with how much saliva is gathering in your mouth. And, hell, you know Ari likes it loud and messy anyway. You try not to moan too obviously as you up the tempo between your own legs.

Footsteps approach again, pausing for a moment when they near you, and you only just manage to keep yourself from bursting into a laugh. Ari doesn't fare as well, whimpering and bracing their hands on the walls of the stall as their thighs start to tremble. They gasp as they come, a helpless sound that shoots straight to your core.

The feet start moving again, shambling swiftly to the door and back out into the venue. And now you really are laughing, drawing back from Ari's cock and gulping air in heaving laughter as you tip onto your ass on the filthy floor. Ari sways at the sudden loss of contact and ends up propped against a wall, laughing almost silently. "Fucker didn't even wash his hands!" they exclaim when they can speak.

You're laughing so hard that tears fill your eyes. You pull your hand back out of your pants, mood shifted enough that it doesn't feel worth it to chase a third. "Says the pot to the kettle!"

"Hey, I may be a fucker but I fully intend to wash my hands," Ari protests playfully.

You waggle your glistening fingers at them. "Guess I should, too."

"You'd better if you don't want the rest of the band asking why your hand smells like crotch." They peel off the condom and look around the stall. Trouble with men's rooms: no trash cans in the stalls. You shrug and they do the same, tossing the used condom onto the floor with the rest of the debris. You'd scold them, but it's probably one of the cleaner things on the floor. They wrangle with their underwear and tuck their packer away before zipping back up. "Fuck, they'll probably want to hang out all night, too. Gonna be uncomfortable as hell in these shorts. Soaking wet, dude."

"You and me both."

They give themself a quick wipe-down with some toilet paper and chuck it into the toilet. "Oh, hey, wait, did you finish?"

You shake your head. "Nah, not this one. I'm good, though."

"You sure? I can stand guard while you take care of business if you want." You shake your head again and they shrug and reach down a hand for you. You take it awkwardly with your clean hand and let them help you to your feet. You take turns washing your hands in the one working sink.

Your legs are still wobbly as you bend to pick up your vest and Ari's shades. Ari doesn't seem too steady on their feet either. You offer them their aviators and they thank you with a smile, giving them a quick rinse and wiping them on their shirt before putting them back on. They tip their head this way and that, checking out their reflection. You sniff your vest and wonder if it would be more hygienic to wear it or to carry it. If it didn't have sentimental value, it'd be better off in the trash. "You're gonna have to do some night laundry," Ari says. "I'll keep you company if you want."

"Sounds like a plan."

They push down their aviators to catch your eyes in the mirror and give you a smirk and a wink. "Maybe we should stay late after our next practice." When you look puzzled, they clarify: "You seemed pretty damn into that scenario of getting fucked on my drum kit. Probably shouldn't *actually* take you onstage in front of everyone, but... might be fun to revisit the fantasy with props. Whatcha think?"

Normally, you don't kiss Ari unless you're actively fucking. But nothing else about tonight has been normal, so you grab them by their shirtfront and pull them into a deep kiss as your reply.

MASTER OF THE HOUSE

Jordan Monroe

Marian had been praying for a slow news day. The Friday morning prior to the Easter recess would be the perfect opportunity for her boss, the Speaker of the House, to announce the party's most ambitious legislative package to date. All the meetings, hearings, phone calls, and vote counts had led to this press conference. As her team prepared to file into the press room, Marian saw that she had a news alert on her personal phone. She opened it and froze.

Senator Gets a Spanking! the tabloid headline read.

Clicking the link, she scanned the sleazy article, hunting for any legitimate information. The platform was one of many opposition outlets that had popped up during the new administration; Marian ignored the hyperbolic adjectives and picked out the words that could hint at facts. *Senator from Massachusetts* and *Marine* and *BDSM* stood out to her. Everything else was suggestion, a lazy tactic that enabled gullible readers to draw their own conclusions.

Though the concerns of the senator from Massachusetts weren't her purview, Marian took this personally.

"Coming, Chief?" one of the press aides asked.

"I've asked you not to call me that, please. And I'll be there in a bit. Go on ahead and make sure the talking points are on the podium."

The aide left, shutting the door behind him, and Marian was finally alone in the oak-paneled office. She took a couple of deep breaths, steadying her nerves. Throughout her eighteen years in national politics, she'd learned a few lessons and gotten out of a scrape here and there, always maintaining her dignity with aplomb. This, though, knocked her off balance.

She didn't care for it.

Marian opened her contacts list and found the name that stirred her most secret yearnings. She pressed the call button and shoved in her earbuds as it rang.

"Pick up, please pick up," she muttered.

The line clicked over and that gruff voice that made her quiver answered. "This is a surprise."

"Adrian, thank you for answering me. Have you seen today's *Hill's Watch*?"

"You know I don't have time to read that rag. Should I have?"

"Yes, you're far too busy with your private security firm. Not to mention your other business."

"Of which you're an integral part."

Marian paused. Now was not the time for banter, much as she enjoyed it, with Adrian Rochester especially. "That's why I called. Someone at *Hill's Watch* is insinuating that the senator from Massachusetts is entangled in a non-vanilla relationship."

Adrian scoffed. "How bored are people, honestly?"

"Bored or not, the details are striking. The article alleges that she's been paying a Marine for scenes."

"And this involves us how?"

"It doesn't, not directly at least. However, the contours of this story are too similar to what we've been up to for my comfort."

"Isn't the package your boss is delivering today supposed to address this?"

"Legalizing sex work and establishing protections for sex workers will not eliminate the public's appetite for salacious details of private matters. You know that as well as I do."

"Marian, because I care for you: you need to stop panicking. First, the senator has plenty of comms folks to swat this away. I'd bet this quarter's earnings that they're laughing about this right now: she's a delight on both social media and in the banking committee, so she's in good hands. Second, while the presidential primaries are going on, no one is going to focus on us. This fabrication is not going to get any oxygen, and no one is going to be looking in our direction. Third, regardless of what anyone thinks of their elected representatives' private business, you are a private citizen."

"A private citizen attached to the Speaker," she retorted.

"But a private citizen, nonetheless. What you do when you're not on the Hill is no one's concern."

Marian sighed. "You're not hearing me: if some intrepid reporter comes across our Tenleytown retreat, they'll inevitably stumble into my involvement and someone with an active imagination will spin my partnership with you to tarnish my boss's reputation. I can't have that. This bill is too important."

"Go to the press conference. Monitor the response. I'll see you tonight at our regular time."

Marian closed her eyes, her spine straightening, the familiar warmth growing in her belly. "Is that a directive, Sir?"

"Yes, pet. For your sanity and for your job, do as you're told."

Marian's hands trembled. She swallowed and answered, "Yes, Master."

"Good girl. Good luck today." With that, the line went dead.

Marian exhaled sharply, adjusted the silk scarf around her neck, a gift from the Speaker two Christmases ago, and slowly made her way to the press room's antechamber. The Speaker pulled her aside. "Everything all right?"

Marian waved her hand in dismissal. "Got distracted by that *Hill's Watch* alert. Did Thomas give you the talking points?"

"They're on the podium. How many votes do we currently have on this?"

"Five stragglers in the caucus but they'll come around with amendments. The evangelicals won't be happy—"

"Well, they never are. What about that alert got your attention? That's not like you."

Marian, who towered over the Speaker even without her Louboutins, lowered her body to whisper, "The details are not dissimilar to what goes on at Piacere."

The Speaker squeezed Marian's arm in reassurance. "You and Adrian are doing good work with Piacere. If there is to be a scandal, it won't come from our office."

Marian smiled weakly. "I greatly appreciate that, ma'am. I don't want to bring a storm to your doorstep."

The Speaker chuckled. "I think we both know that our team can handle anything." She spoke louder. "Shall we make this announcement?"

The team filed into the room, the sounds of camera clicks forcing Marian to focus on the task in front of her.

Adrian hadn't let Marian know that the story made him nervous. Piacere's success, while not dependent on the passage of the bill, would be less assured should it come out that the Speaker's Chief of Staff was, from an unforgiving perspective, both a madam of sorts and a customer of his.

The scenes he and Marian shared were among his most satisfying. Their partnership was one of mutual respect and admiration, which made for a fruitful relationship. He prepared for their sessions with more care than for his other clients, though by only a small margin; he couldn't command the prices he charged without the reputation to match.

The reflection stared back at him: sharp features with a brush of dark evening shadow, burgundy brocade vest containing a crisp unbuttoned white shirt, and fitted black trousers. No tie, of course. They reminded Marian of the halls of Congress, and Piacere was her escape.

Much as it was for a powerful minority in those swampy halls.

The buzzer sounded and he made his way downstairs to the front door. The club was closed to everyone on the nights he and Marian met, members included. Uninterrupted time together was their most precious luxury and they withstood the financial hit to make their nights peaceful. The townhouse was quiet save for the Russian choral music playing softly on the speakers. Marian had long ago told him the voices and harmonies calmed her.

He opened the door to find his partner with a harried look on her face, her large bag pulling her blazer to one side. She stormed in and he shut the door behind her. "Press conference went well today," he remarked, following her to the kitchen.

Marian dropped her bag onto a bar stool, kicked off her heels, and shrugged off her jacket, leaving her wearing nothing save a cerulean blouse and a black pinstripe pencil skirt. She pulled her water bottle from her purse and tilted her head back, taking large gulps. After she capped it, she rolled her shoulders and sighed. "It could have gone worse," she replied.

"You're still bothered by that tabloid, aren't you?"

Her back remained to him. "Logically, I know it shouldn't bother me. We set up our staff with shell companies so they could be further protected from the eyes of the law. Our members are held to the strictest of standards, unlike other establishments."

"Freedom with restraint, that is our operating principle," he said, taking a step closer.

"It troubles me on a deeper level. Bill or no bill, public perception is key. I fear the significance of our work will be swept away should another agitator be more industrious in their discovery. You know how middle America feels about places like this."

Another step. "That won't happen, Marian. You know it won't."

"You can't predict the future."

One more step and he gently placed his hands on her shoulders to steady her. "I can't predict the future, but I can predict how others will behave. Should we get burned, others in far more precarious positions will be caught in the fray."

"You can't be suggesting blackmailing our members?"

"Of course not. I am, however, not above reminding certain members of certain Senate committees of the skeletons in their own closets."

Adrian pressed his thumbs into the sides of Marian's neck. She involuntarily relaxed and tilted her head back into his shoulder, exposing her bare neck.

"You're not wearing your necklace," he whispered.

"I'm sorry, Sir. I didn't want to risk any exposure to you."

"Admirable, but you don't need to protect me. That's my job."

Marian closed her eyes as he wrapped his arms around her waist, pulling her towards him. Her floral perfume barely lingered and he inhaled whatever molecules remained. Adrian deeply cared for her: when they were younger, he had wanted to marry her, but she'd made it clear that marriage wasn't for her. In their own way, they'd come to an understanding. Even so, he never told her that he only played with her.

Marian exhaled slowly and whispered, "Green."

Like a switch being activated, Adrian covered her eyes and pinned her arms behind her torso. He led her roughly to the carefully prepared massage table in the living room. "Eyes closed," he ordered.

"Yes, Sir," she answered.

Adrian unzipped her skirt and slowly pulled it down her legs, taking her pantyhose along with it. He noted her red panties, then ignored them to pull off her blouse and unhook her bra. Dropping it on the floor with one hand, he placed a feather-light kiss on her neck and pressed a hand to the center of her back, pushing her forward. She mounted the massage table and sighed.

With tenderness, Adrian moved her hair to one side, baring Marian's neck. When he pressed his thumbs into the cervical muscles, this time he was firmer. "Leave your hands on the platforms. Don't move them," he commanded in a low voice.

"Yes, Sir," she replied, her voice muffled by the pillow.

Adrian turned to a side table where he had earlier laid out the tools he needed for tonight's session. He'd lit some white candles earlier that now pooled with wax; before he reached for one, he picked up a small bottle of baby oil and poured some in his hand. Turning back to Marian, he rubbed his hands together, warming them, and then he pressed his hands to the backs of her thighs.

Marian hummed into the pillow. Part of what made her his beloved play partner was her open communication with him, an intimacy she shared with so few. Adrian slowly coated her legs with oil, traveling towards the edges of her panties. "You want me to remove these, don't you?"

"In your own time," she mumbled.

Adrian clicked his tongue, pulled down her underwear, and sharply flicked the base of her spine. Marian grunted and flexed her hips upwards. "We've talked about you being polite to the detriment of your desires, pet. Answer me: do you want these gone?"

"Yes, Sir," she said, keeping her hips heighted.

"Good girl," he said, hooking his fingers around her panties and pulling them off her oiled legs, dropping them on the floor.

It was no secret that Marian was blessed with one of the finest asses on the Hill, round and firm from years of traipsing all over town in those deadly heels. Adrian poured more oil in his hands and covered the flesh with it, spreading her cheeks and rubbing his thumbs over the sensitive skin around her puckered hole. Marian moaned and shifted her hips further toward him, but he never indulged her impatience.

She never took time for herself, so with him, time was the ultimate luxury.

Adrian picked up a candle and poured a trail of hot wax on her left leg, starting at the base of her knee. Marian made a purring sound as he continued further up her leg, letting the wax drip down the sides. He held the candle in one hand and in the other, he spread the wax to completely coat her leg. After it was covered, he poured wax on her right leg, making sure it matched the other.

"You'll have to keep your legs still; don't want to let this crack," he said quietly.

Placing the candle back on the table, Adrian reached for the oil again and massaged it into her back, taking care to avoid her dark tresses. He reached around the sides of her body and found the outer slopes of her small breasts, gently covering them with oil. Each time his fingers pressed into her soft flesh, she leaned up, trying to expose whichever nipple was closest. Again, he evaded her trickery.

"Patience, pet."

Marian groaned and he let out a soft chuckle. Trading the oil for another candle, Adrian poured the wax, starting at her lower back and again traveling upwards, spreading the wax to create a thin layer. The wax ran down the sides of her body and he carefully covered the sides of her breasts.

"Christ, this feels good," she said.

"Your pleasure is paramount," he replied, continuing his task. "Again, be still."

Marian obeyed and he returned the candle to the side table. Adrian had an affinity for all types of play, but there was a special place in his dignified, dirty soul for what he had planned next. His next tool was a freshly sharpened paring knife, safely sheathed in its black cover. He picked it up by its wooden handle and slid off the cover, the steel glinting in the candlelight. Adrian walked towards her head and pressed the flat edge of the knife into her neck.

"Now you know why I need you to be still," he whispered.

Marian made a high-pitched sound, reacting to the shock of the cold blade.

"Check in," he said more loudly.

"Green," she answered instantly.

Not questioning her further, Adrian walked to one side of the table and with utmost care, placed the edge of the knife between the now hardened wax on the back of her left thigh. It came off in little flecks, but soon he was able to peel away longer strips. As he focused on his work, his mind drifted to a butterfly emerging from a chrysalis. The creature, much like Marian, was already perfect; the removal of the outer membrane merely allowed Nature to observe the newly exposed beauty.

Adrian stopped where thigh met glute and switched sides, doing the same to the right leg. By now, the table was covered in pieces of white wax, yet he did not brush them away. Periodically, he took the blade between his thumb and forefinger and slid it up, clearing the blade of wax.

When both legs were freshly bared, Adrian began to slowly scrape the wax away from Marian's back, avoiding her buttocks. She hummed and purred, now in complete repose, exactly as he intended. Turning her mind from the day's stresses and towards that transcendental place of inner peace was his sole purpose. Her back cleared of wax, he knelt to her left side, his face level with her body. Adrian placed one hand on the center of her back and carefully pressed the blade to the side of her breast.

Marian moaned and he pressed down on her back more firmly. "Be still, pet."

The wax fell away from her skin and Adrian resisted the urge to touch the soft flesh. He rose and walked to the other side and gently scraped the wax from her right breast. Marian whimpered and he rewarded her with a feather-light finger stroke, caressing the curve. He noticed her fingers clenching the armrests. All thought of the news and press conference, he knew, were absent from her mind; she was now a creature in desperate need of release.

Adrian moved and began to peel the layer of wax away from her ass, leaving the portion closest to her junction. He went back to the table, cleaning the blade along the way, and picked up the final tool in tonight's arsenal: a small yet powerful vibrator. Marian remained still as he took the few steps toward her.

"On your knees, pet. Show me what you know I want to see."

Marian slid her legs up the table and kept her forearms planted on the armrests. Adrian straddled the table behind her and held her hips in his hands. The remaining wax close to her sensitive, pink flesh had cracked. With the steadiest of hands, he scraped it away. The tiny, errant pieces that stubbornly clung to her skin gave him an excuse to run his fingers along her seam. Marian groaned as he made sure every piece was off her skin.

Placing the knife on the floor, he turned on the vibrator and slowly trailed it along her plump outer lips. Marian tilted her hips outward, displaying her glistening cunt. He pressed his thumb on her ass and she cried out.

"You've been so good, pet. Be patient just a little longer."

Marian moaned but didn't say anything; she didn't have to. Adrian swirled the vibrator along her inner lips, keeping his thumb where it was, but lessening the pressure. He decided she'd been in enough delicious agony and held the vibrator on her clit.

"Take what you need," he said.

Holding the vibrator in its place and still pressing on her asshole, Adrian watched as Marian rotated her hips. He heard her panting, the pitch in her little cries getting higher and higher. She gyrated faster, making it

60

difficult for him to maintain his hold on her. Finally, she broke and fell into her orgasm, lifting her head from the pillow and moaning incoherently. After her breathing resumed a steady tempo, he turned off the vibrator and removed his hands from her body.

Adrian exhaled sharply, like he'd just finished a tough gym session. He extracted himself from the table, picked up the knife, and set his tools down on the side table; he'd clean them once he was finished taking care of her. Marian sat up with a slumped posture and he joined her on the table, wrapping an arm around her. She rested her head on his shoulder and sighed heavily.

"Might be some of your best work," she said.

He smiled. "Only the best for you."

Marian took a deep breath and bent down to retrieve her clothes. He was struck by a wild thought; before he could stop himself, he blurted, "Stay with me tonight, Marian."

She straightened and looked at him with skepticism. "You never have guests stay with you."

"You're more than a guest and you know that."

Marian chewed on her lower lip. "Do you think that's wise?"

He shrugged. "Wisdom and wishes rarely coincide."

He reached for her hand. "Please. I'm asking you to stay. I..." he cleared his throat. "I need you to stay. With me. Next to me."

She nodded slowly. "This story has gotten to you too, hasn't it?"

Adrian lowered his eyes and whispered, "Yes."

She squeezed his hand. "Set your alarm for 4 AM. Can't go back tomorrow in the same suit, you know."

He looked at her and kissed her hand. No thanks were needed. He rose and led her away from the table.

Cleaning up and facing the next news cycle could wait until tomorrow.

I CONFESS

EVE RAY

I knelt in the pew, gazing ahead at the flickering red light of the tabernacle. My hands were enmeshed in my rosary beads as I prayed fervently that the Holy Mother would help me make a good confession. I felt my cheeks burn with shame at the thought of the things that I would say. My heart beat faster as I saw the light next to the sign that read Father J Grealish turn to green as the previous penitent closed the confessional door behind her. It was my turn.

I stood up and walked across to the confessional, closing the door, then knelt and blessed myself.

"Bless me, Father, for I have sinned," I began, looking up at the crucifix that hung on the plywood partition above the grille.

Father Grealish's soft, reassuring voice came from behind the partition.

"Sister, have faith in the Lord and His infinite mercy, and tell me the things that are burdening you."

"Father I have sinned greatly in fantasising about Sister Agatha, a new nun in the convent. I lie in bed at night, knowing that her cell is next to mine, that only a thin wall divides us, I fantasise about her coming in naked, her hair shaken loose. I see her cunt set in a luxuriant growth of hair, I imagine her climbing on to my bed, sinking her face into my hair, kissing me, then I feel her tongue on my vulva, feel her lips clamping my pussy lips as I rub my clit, before she pushes my hand aside, and tongues me until I come."

"And that is all in your imagination, and only your imagination?"

"Yes, Father, it is a fantasy but, last week as I worked with Sister Agatha in the laundry, and we were folding sheets, I touched her breasts. I left my hand there for a second and then, as we loaded the washing machine, I touched the nape of her neck, kissed it. She turned, she looked a bit startled, then she smiled and took my hand. I went to the toilet, sat on the seat playing with myself. I was wet."

"Have you fantasised about anyone else, my Sister?"

"Yes, Father, I have fantasised about you."

"And how?"

"It was at Mass last Sunday, Father, as I knelt at the communion rail and you came towards me holding the pyx. You stood before me, held up a Host, and it turned into a cock as you held it. You said, 'The Cock of Christ' and I sucked and sucked as spunk, sweet as honey, flowed out to fill my mouth. I felt that I was wet. I felt my clit gorged with blood, felt it rubbing against my knickers, and I had to pretend to go to confession, to play with myself, and I held you before me, in all your masculine beauty, how you lifted your vestments to takeout your huge cock, push it into my mouth, make me suck and suck until it hardened, grew big, and you arched your back and I swallowed another load of your come.

"Then you threw me back into the hard convent bed, took a knife and sliced my habit down the front, sliced my bra, my knickers, and I was suddenly a woman, an aroused woman, so wet my juices were leaking out and trickling down my inner thigh, gagging, just gagging to be fucked, fucked hard, fucked roughly so that it hurt and I pleaded for you to stop. But you didn't. You rammed me mercilessly, you were cold, unfeeling, you were what I needed, what I deserved. I am not a nun any more, Father, I am a dirty slag, I have betrayed my vows. I deserve to be locked in a brothel, a painted whore, serving stinking men who…"

I began to cry. I was wallowing in self-abasement. I was wet again. I prayed for my penance to be severe, thousands of Hail Marys to be recited kneeling on spikes, or on a cold, tiled floor so that I writhed in agony. I didn't need to reach inside my knickers. My clit rubbing against the rough convent underwear was enough to bring me to climax.

As the orgasm shuddered through me, I looked up at the crucifix. I saw Christ glowing in bright light, saw blood run from his side, saw come colour his plain white loin cloth, which lifted from his body as his erection grew bigger.

"Oh Christ, oh my heavenly husband, fuck me, fuck me!!"

I fell back, exhausted. As I lay on the floor, Father Grealish walked round from behind the partition and stood over me.

"My Sister, you need to be quieter. Just think of the scandal if one of the simple faithful were to hear your confession."

"I'm sorry, Father."

He knelt beside me. He cradled my head in his hand.

"If one of the simple faithful were to hear that, it would cause them much pain and confusion. Holy Mother Church enjoins sexual continence and chastity, but only for them. For those of us that God almighty has seen fit to enlighten with His wisdom, sex is a celebration of His creation, of He who saw fit to create the vulva, once just an idea in His infinite mind, now made flesh through His providence, for the enjoyment of those who serve Him in the priestly caste."

"I don't need to be ashamed of my feelings, then, Father?" The corners of Father's mouth turned upward, as if he understood my pleading—my desire— to be punished and have my fantasies become reality.

"You have sinned greatly and must do penance."

"How, Father?" I grinned.

"You will say 2,000 Hail Marys while kneeling on a cold stone floor."

"So many, Father?" I asked, in a mixture of horror and delight.

"So many. But first, you are to receive the Cock of Christ. Does this excite you?"

I nodded yes, mouth agape.

He lifted off his cassock and dropped his trousers. His boxers were bulging already, and his huge erection soon burst through the slit. The tip was a veined purple mountain peak, slippery wet, glistening in the light that shone down from above Christ on his cross. Something began to drip from the end.

I squirmed.

I had never seen a penis so close before. I stared in fascination, frozen by the enormity of what I was about to do. It was in this church that I had taken my vows. Here, I had walked in, in a bridal dress, carrying a small bouquet, to be married to Christ.

Here that I had been taken into a side room to be dressed in the heavy brown habit of the Order of The Sisters of Perpetual Abstinence, and have my head covered with the black wimple. Here that my hair had been cut before I took the veil. Here that I had felt arousal as I spoke the vows. I am sure I came as I spoke the vow of chastity, as I come every night, speaking it in my bare convent cell as I grind against the coarse bed sheets, wishing for Christ to come to me, to make me His, as every wife craves the body of her husband.

"Sister," began Father Grealish, "it is the teaching of the Church that the priest, in exercise of his ministry, acts in the person of Christ. My cock is the cock of Christ, the come you will drink, sweet as milk and honey as only the Come of Christ can be. Come and drink, and be healed."

"Please Father, please heal with me your cock and your sweet, sweet milk?" My insides burned.

He took a step forward.

I eagerly took it in my mouth. I rocked gently forward on my knees, taking in his whole length, covering it with saliva, sucking and licking, as I had once read you were supposed to do. I heard him moan softly, felt his body relax even as his penis swelled in my mouth and grew harder. I rocked back and let his cock slide almost out, with just the tip left in my mouth. I ran my tongue around the end, and he moaned again, this time a little louder. Then I rocked forward again, once more taking the full length into my mouth. And then I felt it shudder and he moaned out loud, "Oh Christ, Oh Christ!"

My mouth filled with salty cream, which I tried to swallow, but there was so much that it ran out of my mouth and dribbled down my chin, and onto the brown habit of perpetual chastity. I thought he was finished, but he quickly pumped his hips and pushed rhythmically, and I choked as my mouth filled with more come.

He stopped and withdrew, looking at me as I knelt before him on all fours, struggling to get my breath back. *I was healed*, I thought. I was forgiven in the most delicious way.

"Sister, the first stage of your spiritual healing is complete. You have drunk the sweet Come of Christ. Now you are to revolve into your body. Stand before the grille, bend over so that you kiss the feet of Christ on His cross."

I did as I was told, feeling an even greater heat rising inside me.

"Now, Sister, you are to lift your habit, let your knickers fall to the floor and part your bum cheeks with your hands."

Again, I did as I was told. He walked behind me, and I heard him take a step towards me. I felt moisture building between my thighs. He grabbed my hips roughly, and entered me with some force.

I felt a frisson of fear as I realised that this was the moment I had broken my vow of perpetual virginity, here in the confessional, the place of forgiveness and mercy. I was damned, I was doomed. But I didn't care. Maybe Father Grealish was right, and it was God's Holy Will that he should fuck me here.

"It is the Cock of Christ that has invaded you, Sister, with all the spiritual gifts that accrue from submitting."

And I leant forward, reached for the crucifix, kissed the feet, imagined them sweet with the nard that Mary had anointed them with, even as the sweat and blood of His precious death congealed on His skin. And then my lips touched the loincloth, my mouth lingering over His crotch, as I shut my eyes and focused on my fucking.

Father's thrusts were hard and brutal. His final push rammed my face against the crucifix, and I am sure, even now, that I felt the cock burst free from the loincloth, fill my mouth and ejaculate milk and honey that I swallowed greedily.

"Fuck me, Father, fuck me harder. Fuck me!"

He placed a hand over my mouth and hissed, "Be quiet, this is our secret. Can you imagine the scandal if the simple faithful found out what we are called to? That we practice spiritual chastity only through debauchery of the flesh? That this is His divine purpose?" Father paused for a moment. "You still need further healing. This time I am going to fuck you up the bottom."

"Bottom?"

"Three fucks, one for each person of the Trinity. The Come of Christ must dribble out of three orifices. Only that way can you be cleansed of your great sin."

I bent over again, leant against the partition and clenched my buttocks. Father Grealish spat into his hands and rubbed saliva around my hole. Now, both fear and desperate desire filled me.

"Relax," he said softly, "don't fight this. It will be a thing of beauty. This is the ultimate giving of yourself to Christ, the consummation of your marriage to Him."

He pushed a finger inside, gently, slowly. My reflex was to tighten my muscles around the finger and resist the invasion. But I wanted this. So I relaxed, breathed in deeply, prayed that the Lord would give me fortitude to endure this. Endure? No, enjoy. I had to enjoy this as I had enjoyed the nectar in my mouth, how I had felt deep joy as he fucked me, as…

He slid in. This was quick: he was clearly tired, too. There were two brief thrusts: his vigour had gone. He withdrew, and I sank to the floor exhausted, fucked nearly senseless. I could only see his flaccid member that had been so recently huge and full of come. I was sated and tired. He became a blur as I cried tears of happiness. My inner thighs were wet, wet with the Come of My Lord, wet with my juices. I would be a good wife to Christ, my body would be His whenever He needed it, I would refuse Him nothing. He would give Me everything.

I lay on the floor, used and spent. But I felt a deep joy. Father Grealish stood over me, and said the words of absolution, *"Absolvo te in nomine Patris et Filii et Spiriti Sancti."*

I began to cry. I quickly rearranged my habit and wimple. Hoping no one would see the come stain, which was even bigger than I had imagined, I hurried out of the church, almost forgetting to genuflect as I passed in front of the altar where the red tabernacle lamp was flickering, just as it had done in that distant age, over an hour before, when I was still a virgin.

In bed that night, I reflected on the day. I thought of Father Grealish's fat, veined, cock, saw the foreskin pulled back, the bell-end glistening, a harpoon ready to

70

spear me with delight again. As I rubbed my clit, my thoughts turned to Sister Agatha, asleep in her cell just a few feet away from me. I visualised her small, firm breasts, the bush I had glimpsed in the shower and into which I wanted to plunge my face. And now I knew what I had to do when I did. I knew that I had to sin and sin boldly. I needed confession. I needed it soon.

I got out of bed and put on my slippers. I went out into the corridor. Sister Agatha's door was slightly ajar, as if to invite me in. I peered round the door and, for a minute, watched her as she lay in bed, the blanket pulled up around her chin. I had the impression she was only pretending to sleep. Then she opened her eyes and looked at me. I went in and shut the door gently behind me.

IF A TREE FALLS

Louise Kane

I took a bite of crusty bread smeared with creamy brie and fig jam, falling back onto the checkered picnic blanket spread beneath me. I chewed carefully as the noise of the other parkgoers washed over me. Content in that way only a sunny afternoon full of good food and company could make me, I swallowed the bread and blinked drowsily up at Mary.

Leaning back on her elbows, with her corduroy-clad legs crossed at the ankles, she looked like a studious doctoral student taking a quick break from her dissertation to enjoy the summer sun. A *handsome* doctoral student, with a penchant for wearing black leather boots even in warm weather. I lingered on her boots before moving to her hands and bare forearms—burnt already, though summer had only begun—and finally landing on her face.

To find her already staring at me.

My cheeks flushed as she steadily held my gaze with honey-brown eyes. A year of picnics and kissing and loving and kneeling meant that, even in a crowded park, that look inspired immediate deference—and arousal. With a smirk that told me she knew exactly what she was doing, Mary lazily brushed a thumb against my right nipple through the thin fabric of my silk shirt.

I gasped, eyebrows rising in playful affront even as heat sparked in my stomach. Mary knew how much I enjoyed playing in public—and luckily for me, she had a penchant for taking advantage of that knowledge. She responded with another brush, casual enough to convince myself that onlookers would think she was only rubbing soothing lines into my chest. I held my limbs tight, a trickle of sweat wending down the center of my chest as all playfulness slipped away, my peaked nipples offering unassailable evidence of desire to anyone who cared to look.

"Do you want to go on an adventure, pretty girl?" asked Mary, thumb moving steadily.

"Yes," I whispered. "But I also don't want you to stop."

"I promise you'll like what comes next even better," said Mary, twisting my nipple sharply. My cunt leapt at the surge of pain and the promise it made, but she'd already dropped her hand. "Now help me clean up."

I allowed myself a moment to sift through the headiness her touch had ignited in me before sitting up. Trash was collected, leftovers were wrapped and stored away, and the blanket was quickly folded. By the time we were done, I was almost human again—although I whimpered every time my hardened nipples brushed against my button-up.

Mary grabbed my hand, sparking a conversation about nothing as she led me away from the grassy field and toward a more forested section of the park. I squeezed her hand, aching to ask what she had planned. That would be pointless though; Mary enjoyed the flourish of a reveal too much to tell me anything useful. In our time together, I'd learned to relish the heightened eroticism of the unknown.

Eventually Mary's pace slowed, and we stopped in front of a group of trees so tightly packed together that I could barely see through them. Before I was able to ask what we were doing here, Mary pulled me through a small opening and then, somehow, we were alone.

We stood in the center of a copse of smooth-trunked trees, strains of conversation and laughter slowly filtering into my awareness. The dense foliage served as a natural barrier between us and the outside world, obscuring sight and muffling sound enough to create the illusion of privacy. We were in a room all our own—even if there was no lock on the door. She could do anything to me, and anyone might stumble in and see.

It made me unbearably wet.

Mary pushed me roughly against the lone tree in the middle of the clearing, and I gasped with surprised delight. My silk shirt did nothing to protect me from the coarse bark. In a distant part of my mind, I wondered if my back would be patterned with it once we were done.

"You like to be looked at," said Mary, tracing a finger down my side. "Don't you, pretty girl?"

"Yes," I said, breathless with arousal and the embarrassment of how much I liked to be looked at. How much I wanted her to fuck me right here, right now, with no regard for whether we got caught. Perhaps because of exactly that possibility.

"Good," she said, dropping her hand to my shirt collar. "I plan to show you off."

I blushed deeper as her eyes left mine and she slowly unbuttoned my shirt. Undoing the button beneath my tits, she slid a hand inside to grab my right breast just as a loud peal of laughter rang out beyond our haven. My stomach dropped as my eyes darted over her shoulder, any earlier bravado disappearing at the first notion of actually being caught—and the reminder that reality was never as simple as fantasy.

After seconds passed without anyone barreling into the clearing, I blew out a shaky breath and returned my focus to Mary. She hadn't noticed my brief terror, too intent on lavishing attention on my tits. Good. I could do this. I *wanted* this. Just because reality wasn't as simple, didn't mean it wasn't as fun. I sank into her touch as the flame inside me rekindled.

"Girls like you love to be played with, don't they?" she asked, kneading my chest. "Even better when it's in public, where people can see. A slut like you just can't help herself, can she?"

"No," I breathed, the last of my worry forgotten in the wake of her words and the ache they ignited in my cunt.

"No, I didn't think so." Mary pinched my nipple hard enough to elicit a cry, but I swallowed it before it could escape. Shivering against the tree, I breathed through my nose trying to regain some composure. "Good thing I'm here to help."

She undid another shirt button, and another, until she could push apart the fabric to expose my tits to the open air. I shook with nervous need as her clothed body covered my nakedness from the outside world and her hands cupped my breasts.

Then she stepped back.

My hands stuttered at my sides, the impulse to cover myself warring with my choice to trust her enough to keep me safe. I clenched them into fists against my thighs, forcing them down. Terrified and exhilarated, I waited for whatever came next.

"Touch yourself," said Mary.

I flexed my fingers and brought both hands up to my tits, eyes steadily on hers as I squeezed hard enough to bruise. I closed my eyes as I lost myself in the feeling—pinching and grabbing and kneading and holding—knowing both that she was staring and that anyone else might catch a glimpse of me through the trees. The game was not to get caught, but that didn't mean the fantasy of someone stumbling upon us didn't make my blood burn hotter.

Then her hands replaced mine.

"Such a good girl." Mary's fingernails dug into sensitive flesh so slowly that it took a moment for the pain to catch up. "I bet I could leave you here for hours with only the direction to touch yourself, and you'd happily obey. In fact, you'd probably hope someone would catch you, so that you'd have something more to play with."

I whimpered, desire thrumming through me at the fantasy she was weaving with her words, even as I wondered how she'd read my mind as easily as the initials carved into the tree at my back. She smirked at my wide eyes, and I knew I'd misunderstood. She hadn't read me. Rather, she'd thrown out the fishing line with a bit of bait on the hook—and I'd been caught.

"That's what I thought," said Mary, wedging her knee between my legs so that it pressed against my clit. I bit down on a groan. "A dirty little slut like you can't help herself. Of course, you'd prefer it were me inside you, but that doesn't mean you're picky enough to say no to anyone else willing to fill those pretty little holes, does it?"

"No," I whispered, accompanied by the slightest shake of my head. "It doesn't."

"Lucky for you, I have a certain fondness for greedy sluts." Mary shifted forward, pinning me against the tree. I moaned, deep in my throat, and began moving on her thigh in search of the friction I desperately needed. "Do you want me to fuck you?"

I whined, deep in my throat. "Please."

"What would you do for it?"

"Anything."

"That's a dangerous answer, slut," said Mary, grin going hard. "Unzip your pants."

I suffered a moment's hesitation at the state of undress that would leave me in, but then I hurriedly undid my zipper and slid my jeans down my hips to give her easier access to my cunt—which she blessedly took. With one hand gripping me hard around the neck, she shoved the other one down my pants to cup my mound.

"Someone's soaking," said Mary, a tinge of breathlessness belying her wry delivery. "That desperate to feel me inside you?"

"Very," I said, wriggling my hips. "Please."

"Well, I suppose I've played with my prey long enough."

Mary groaned as she slid a finger into me, and I cried out too loudly for where we were but too lost to care. She shoved my face into her shoulder to muffle my moans as I scrabbled against her shirt, desperate for something to sink into to keep from floating away. She added another finger, and I yelped despite my best efforts.

"Be quiet now, sweet girl," said Mary, going still inside me. "I know you like to be watched, but we wouldn't want to get in trouble, now would we?"

"No," I whispered, distantly aware of the truth of her words even as my cunt pulsed with the thought of strangers' eyes on me. Mary's fingers thrust into me as I fantasized about them watching through the branches. Her teeth sunk into my neck as I imagined those same strangers wondering what else a slut like me might do for them. My chest tightened as I imagined exactly what my answer to that question would be.

"Fuck," breathed Mary, voice tight with desire. "Turn around. Hands on the tree. Now."

I did as she said and was rewarded with her pushing down my jeans and underwear to my knees. I was too far gone to remember the earlier fear that had thrummed through me at the possibility of actually being caught. All I could think about was how to get her inside me. I whined, pushing my ass toward her and, finally finally finally, she shoved three fingers deep into me.

"Shit." I bit down hard on my lip to keep any other sounds from escaping as Mary pushed deep and fast and hard into my cunt, pressing me into the tree with each thrust. The rough bark against my tits, my thighs, my stomach only heightened the feeling of her between my legs until all I cared about was making sure she didn't stop until she'd drawn everything from me. Until she'd left me with legs so weak that I couldn't stand without the tree to lean on.

Then she was hitting that perfect spot that would've had me screaming if we were anywhere but here, and I rocked against her as my nails dug into the bark in front of me. Mary's groans filled my ear, quickening the steady build of an orgasm made sharper by the knowledge that we could be caught at any moment and my orgasm lost if we were. But we weren't... and then I was biting my bicep hard enough to bruise and it felt so unbelievably good and I was coming all over her hand and down my thighs and into the dirt beneath me.

I sagged against the tree, breathing deeply through my nose as Mary withdrew from my cunt. She wiped my wetness on the insides and backs of my thighs before running a soft finger down my neck. I turned slowly, grasping the front of her shirt to end our scene with a kiss. She lingered on my lips, soft and sweet—but only for a moment.

"Oh, you're not done yet, sweet thing," said Mary, voice somehow steady as she pulled away. "Get on your hands and knees and thank me properly."

I whimpered, heat rekindling in my stomach as I dropped to the leaf and stick–strewn ground and crawled the short distance to her black leather boots. Wrapping my hands around the heel of her left boot, I tongued the leather covering her toes and lost myself in the effort of showing her how I loved her. She moaned, low and long, as I mouthed the leather upper and massaged her ankle and calf. I was both lost in the act and beyond it. The smallest of whimpers escaped me as I returned to the toe of her boot, pressing open-mouthed kisses to it while I breathed in its leathery scent.

"The other one," said Mary, voice hoarse with unspent desire.

Framing her right boot with my bare thighs, cunt displayed for all the world to see, I arched my neck to find the places on her boot that were hardest to reach. When I was at her feet, there was nothing else. No strangers to worry about, no hard ground to distract me—just endless gratitude for the self that I was able to be with Mary. I would lick her boots forever if it meant proving the depth of that gratitude.

"That's enough, pretty girl," said Mary, voice soft. "Time to get dressed."

I leaned back, so lost in the haze of worship and a thorough fucking that it took a moment for her words to register. And then, quickly, the reality of the situation returned in full color. I was on my knees in the middle of a public park, pants and underwear around my knees, tits fully out, and anyone could walk in at any time.

"Oh my god," I said, giggling as I clumsily pulled up my jeans and rebuttoned my shirt. I shot Mary a toothy grin. "That was...definitely an adventure."

"Told you that you'd like it," said Mary, helping me to my feet and brushing off errant leaves before pulling me into their arms for a soft kiss and a hard hug. We breathed in sync with each other as she rubbed small circles into my back. "Do you feel good?"

"Very much," I said, smiling into her chest. "All the park adventures, please. What's summer without a little public fun, after all?"

"That's a silly question," said Mary, planting a kiss on top of my head. "What's a forest without trees?"

AGAIN TOMORROW

Elliot Sawyer

I ensconce myself behind a doily-covered dessert table to escape a pair of prying eyes. I hadn't thought my black dress inappropriate for the occasion, and yet some aunt twice or thrice removed has been shooting disapproving glances at my neckline all night. It's a bit tight, I'll admit, but I prefer my clothes form-fitting. Perhaps it's not the dress that's got her face pinched in a dour mask. It could be the tendrils of blue hair that fall around my collar bones.

"You look like a mermaid," my mother informed me, last time I'd called home over video chat.

I knew she hadn't meant it as a compliment. But I smiled and, with a conspiratorial wink, replied, "Thanks."

The table is heavily laden with towering confections of chocolate and melting ice-cream, and cousin Felecia's untouched sweet potato pie that's mostly marshmallows, and so I think I'll be able to hide for a while. I am almost immediately proven incorrect.

"Bri! There you are."

I prepare myself as my mother's wife, Naomi, rounds the far side of the table. I don't consider Naomi a parent, as she and my mother have only been married the last couple of years. She wasn't in my life as a child. But I can tell they are happy together, so I make an effort when I am home. It doesn't make it easier for us to find things to talk about.

"Oh. Naomi, hi." I say in a tone that suggests I hadn't noticed her before just now, when in fact we'd both been suffering this family reunion for hours.

"Your mom really knows how to throw a party," Naomi says.

"Mmm." I agree, noncommittally.

"We're so glad you could make it. I know you've been so busy with grad school," Naomi tries. "Literature, that's got to be interesting."

I try to think of something stimulating and intelligent to say on the subject. "Yeah," I say while I think, and the end of the word stretches out to "ahhh." I close my mouth to cut off the obnoxious sound. Before I can say anything else, my cousin Felecia walks up, waddling because of the baby bump.

"A master's. Wow. Too much education won't do you any favors, though. Experience. That's what you need." She looks at the untouched sweet potato pie, then looks away again, as though not noticing no one has eaten any.

"I like school," I say. Because it's true.

"I can see that." She sighs, an overblown, world-weary sigh, rubbing her swollen midriff. "It's too bad we can't all fritter away our time in a classroom. One day you'll have real responsibilities, then you'll understand. The real world isn't like the classroom."

My answering smile is brittle, but I don't care enough about her or her opinions to muster the effort of actual offense.

"I see you brought two men," Felecia says. I follow her eyes to two young men standing near the back of the dining room, and my smile softens to one of affection. Danny, slight with wavy hair, wearing a sweater vest. Javier, tall and striking to the point that it can be distracting.

"Are they friends of yours? Is one a boyfriend?" asks Naomi, seeing a way back into the conversation.

Ah. Here we go. "No," I say. "One of them isn't my boyfriend."

They both look curious at the emphasis I place on the word *one*.

"They're both my boyfriends," I finish.

Felecia's answering stare is one of naked confusion, and Naomi's is one of awkwardness.

"Both?" asks Felecia.

I nod, mildly amused at her struggle with the concept. She looks at tall, umber-skinned Javier, at Danny's soft, gentle smile. Then she looks at me. Back at them again. Back at me.

"How can they both be your boyfriends?" she asks.

"I'm dating both of them. Both of them are dating me." It's as simple as that, really.

She looks at the men again, how close together they stand. At the way they seem to pull towards one another, heads bent away from the rest of the party conspiratorially. I see understanding flash like a harsh light in Felecia's eyes as Javier places a hand tenderly on Danny's shoulder.

ELLIOT SAWYER

Her jaw stiffens. Something hard replaces her usual condescension. She seems deeply offended, as though my dating choice persecutes her. Confusion, I've gotten from people before. Sometimes disdain. But what always surprises me is the personal anger some people feel at the idea of multiple partners.

"That'... quite a unique situation you have there," she says in a tone that's so overly saccharine it comes out clipped.

I shrug, trying not to take too much pleasure in how I've scandalized her.

"Well," she says, still in that falsely lilting voice. "It seems my *husband*," she utters the word as though it were a talisman against debauchery, "needs help with the twins. Perhaps I'll get to meet your... friends... later." She sweeps away, with surprising haughtiness for someone carting around a nearly fully-formed human inside her.

For a moment, we are left with silence. I feel a flash of empathy for Naomi's discomfort. She'd been making an effort to connect with me, and I know I don't make it easy.

"It's really not as indecent as people think," I say. I know the thought of multiple partners is usually synonymous with cheating. But that's not how polyamorous relationships work. We are all honest with each other. We all care for each other.

"I'm just taking it in." Naomi says. "So," she looks at the men. "They both date you. Do they date each other, too?"

"Yes, actually." I feel extremely lucky at my triad. "It started off as just Danny and I for a while. Then Danny went to Argentina for a semester. Javier kind of... followed him back."

It had been good with Danny. And when Javier came into the picture, it only got better.

"Oh, so… that didn't create problems? With Danny and you?"

I smile, thinking back. Danny had been acting strange since returning. Nervous and guilty. But I quickly pried the problem from him.

"I know we're both bi," Danny had said, wringing his hands. We were in the living room of my tiny apartment just off campus at the time. "But we never discussed what would happen… what would happen if," he'd trailed off. "I fell for Javi. But I still love you. I don't know what to do, Bri."

At first, I'd been at a loss as well. Was I losing Danny to Javier?

But then I'd met Javier. Tall, handsome Javier with his serene smile. I saw how good they were together. All my intimidation melted away.

And then, I fell for Javier, too.

"Not really. I knew that if I wanted to continue my relationship with Danny, I needed to let him also be with Javier. It was awkward the first couple times we all hung out, but I could see how much they cared about each other. And then Javier and I grew to care about each other, too. We've all considered ourselves together since then."

Naomi nods slowly. "It's… hard for me to imagine not getting jealous, were I in a situation like that. But I suppose if you all care about each other equally…" She trails off, not quite knowing how to finish her thought.

I appreciate her effort to understand. It's more than many others have offered.

***

Back at the hotel, I peel off the tight dress with a sigh of satisfaction. I step under the glorious spray of the shower and let the hot water run in rivulets over my body. I soap my hair with fragrant shampoo as the bathroom fills with steam.

The party had been long and tedious, but it's over now, and I can be alone with Javier and Danny. I hope they will join me in the shower. But, as time goes on, and the heat of the water warms my skin, they do not come. So I step out of the shower. I don't put on the waiting robe. Walking out into the cooler air beyond the bathroom is a delicious shock.

I find Danny and Javier already on the bed. Danny's sweater, undershirt, jeans and socks are in a rumpled pile on the floor. Danny's eyes are closed, chin tilted to the ceiling as though in supplication, lips slightly parted. Javier lies next to him, eyes wicked as he goes about his task. That's the part of Javier I fell for first, my body anyway: the mischievous glint in his eyes when he stripped either of us naked.

I watch as Javier plants kisses on Danny's neck, his hand slowly moving up and down inside Danny's boxers, the only thing he still has on. I feel the heat from the shower sink in deeper at the sight. Without pausing, Javier uses his free hand to indicate the empty space on the bed next to him.

I take a seat next to him, leaning against Javier's sturdy frame as he continues to pleasure Danny. As I watch, Javier's lips move lower, kissing the bud of Danny's nipple. Danny squirms, letting out a pleading sound as Javier's tongue flicks out to taste. His tongue is followed by a flash of teeth biting gently down on the sensitive flesh. Danny's hips buck and he groans, looking at Javier with hazy eyes.

I reach over and help Danny take the boxers off, tossing them down on the floor with the other clothes. I also help Javier take off his coat and shirt. He must have set upon Danny the instant we'd returned, without bothering with his own clothes.

Javier gives me a quick kiss of thanks before leaning down over Danny again. He kisses his hips, and his inner thighs. Danny pants. Javier runs his tongue over Danny's lower stomach, back and forth, back and forth, getting closer and closer to the place that will give Danny the truest pleasure. I tug Javier's hair, chastising him for being a tease, and he chuckles. The sound rippling over Danny's flesh causes him to let out a strangled sound.

As Javier positions himself to lie between Danny's spread thighs, I lie down on my side as well, closer to Danny's face. Blue hair hanging forward, I lean over and kiss him. He kisses me back, desperately, needing to take some of the control. His tongue slides into my mouth, and I allow him to pull my face closer.

I can tell Javier has finally given him what he wants when his breath hitches against my lips. His head rolls back, and he cries out. I look down to see that Javier has taken Danny in his mouth. His head bobs up and down, up and down, slowly as Danny whimpers and groans.

I bite my lip, finding that my hips are grinding against the bed. I hadn't known I would enjoy the sight of two men together until the first time the three of us slept together.

Heat pools in my belly as Javier's hands rub Danny's thighs. Javier pauses to slick a finger before lowering it between Danny's legs. He takes Danny back into his mouth. A moment later he presses the wet finger forward, and I watch it slide inside.

Danny and I moan at the same time. As Javier's finger moves in and out of Danny, I shiver. I love watching Danny reduced to a quivering mess. I lean over as Danny moans, taking back his mouth with my own, wanting to absorb some of the pleasure. The indecent sound of Javier's mouth on Danny's flesh fills the room, but is soon overtaken by Danny's moans. He is close. I lean back to watch as Javier's finger pumps faster and faster, in and out of Danny. When Javier adds a second finger, it's all over.

Danny orgasms.

Javier leans back, wiping his mouth. He looks at me.

"Ready for more?" I ask.

He laughs, as though the answer should be obvious, but leans back to show me the hardness between his legs.

"I want to go fast," I say. I am already close from watching them, and I don't want any of Javier's tortuous teasing.

"Good." He flicks his wrist, giving me a jaunty come-hither gesture. I crawl over, careful not to disturb the recovering Danny. When I reach Javier, I shove his chest playfully, and he falls prone onto the bed.

I swing a leg around, mounting him.

"Hmmm." He groans at how effortlessly I slide him inside of me. I'd been ready for this all night, and walking in on them together has made me desperate for it.

I rock my hips at a rapid pace, not bothering to start slow. Javier grips my waist tightly, as first letting me take total control. As time goes on, my thrusts grow desperate, and he raises his hips as I lower them, meeting in the middle.

The sounds of slapping flesh and our panting fills the room. I've never been much of a moaner, but I often breathe so hard I get dizzy. I feel the light-headedness coming on now, feel the first prickling of the orgasm ramping to its peak.

"God, you're beautiful," he says. "You're both so beautiful."

I look over to see Danny watching us. He's hard again, after only a few minutes, and he has his hands between his own legs, stroking. He makes eye contact with me, and I see how much he enjoys the sight of Javier and I together, the same as I enjoy the two of them together. This undoes me.

I groan and rock my hips furiously two, three more times and I feel myself hit my peak. Javier finishes at the same time, and we both pant for a minute or two, me slumped on his chest.

After a moment I roll off, and the three of us lie naked, side by side. I feel a bit sleepy, but Danny apparently has other plans. He pulls Javier to him again, and the two exchange kisses. Javier runs his hands through Danny's hair, and Danny kisses at Javier's neck. I watch, only half paying attention as the kissing slowly moves from romantic to needy. Danny's hands slip between Javier's legs, willing him to get hard again.

Javier obliges.

His stamina never ceases to amaze me.

Soon, Javier is spreading Danny's legs again. He is crawling between them, but this time it's not a finger that pins Danny down. I watch as the hardness that had fifteen minutes earlier been inside of me, slides inside of Danny. As Danny wraps his legs around Javier's waist. As Javier rocks inside Danny slowly, so painstakingly slowly.

The two of them are so tender. Javier grips Danny's thighs, hoisting them over his shoulders, so he can push in deeper. He angles himself to a position that will give Danny the greatest pleasure. Since we have been doing this together for months now, he finds the spot quickly. Danny cries out. Javier groans, gritting his teeth. His rakish expression is replaced with one of need. He slams his hips down faster now, and the bed shakes with his thrusts.

I could keep watching. I could pleasure myself again. But I am tired, and there is always tomorrow. And so I turn away, so they will not tempt me. I pull a blanket over me, as the sound of the two men making love fills the room. It is a familiar sound.

"Good night," I tell them, though they are not listening.

It doesn't matter. Tomorrow we will wake up and do it all again.

GUILT FOR TWO

Dilo Keith

I awoke with a naked redhead in my arms and my cock nestled between his butt cheeks, the familiarity making it no less special. Kyler, my housemate and best friend, was still asleep. More than fuck buddies and less than romantic partners, we often slept and had sex together when not busy with dates or my two dominants. My only complaint about serving two men was not getting to spend more time with Kyler, who was at home nearer the vanilla end of the sex spectrum than I could ever be on a permanent basis. I nuzzled the back of his neck and kissed him awake.

Faced with a busy day, we couldn't linger in bed. Eliot and Michael, my doms, had dropped off Eliot's car so I could use it to follow Kyler to the repair shop and then take him to work at Eliot's place. Kyler had worked for Eliot almost a year, and was the one who had introduced me to him and his husband Michael, a man almost twice my age. We'd get my car, which was also laid up, later in the day. If we had time, I planned to drop off my boots for repair so I'd have them back for the big party on Saturday. I loved being publicly displayed, dressed to please my masters and having appreciative onlookers witness my submission.

I checked with Kyler around eleven-thirty to see if we'd be able to combine lunch and picking up my car. With the workload under control, Eliot had no problem with our plans for an extended lunch.

We were almost at the car repair shop when Eliot called Kyler with the hope that we were close to returning. Somewhere in the car, he had left a flash drive with an image required for last-minute changes a customer needed by 1:30 that afternoon. For that and other reasons, a quick return became essential.

"We can get my car tonight," I offered.

"No need, we pass right by. Okay if we just drop you off? The car's definitely ready, right?"

"Yes. That'll work. Eliot's fine with you driving."

A huge line of red taillights greeted us after we turned the next corner.

"Can you see if there's an accident or something?" Kyler asked.

"I can't see anything past the curve."

"We can turn on Oak Street and go around; it'll be quicker."

"Left turns aren't allowed there," I said. "It's also hard to see traffic coming."

He made several arguments in favor of making the left anyway and managed to persuade me. Unfortunately, I misjudged the available space and the car I pulled in front of had to slam on the brakes.

Thud. A metallic one.

"Oh, fuck. Are you okay?" I asked.

"Yeah, it wasn't much impact, but I doubt the car is fine."

"Double fuck." The fact that the guy who hit us was probably going too fast didn't make me feel less guilty. "Oh, great, the cops, too."

After exchanging all the necessary documentation, I dialed Eliot's number with a shaking hand.

"Where are you? I thought you'd be back by now."

He sounds miffed. "We had a little problem, but things are okay now. We're ten minutes away." *There, that sounded calm enough.*

"Just get your butts back here."

Great, he had to mention butts.

***

That evening, I called Kyler on my way there and received the good news that Eliot had given no sign of knowing about the accident. Relieved, I continued mentally revising and rehearsing my confession, contemplating how to downplay the part about Kyler urging me to make the turn. There was no point in getting Eliot upset with him too.

Eliot greeted me with, "In my office. Both of you."

Shit fuck damn.

"Have a seat, boys. Is there anything you want to tell me?"

I guessed I wouldn't be using my carefully planned speech and didn't say anything.

Eliot filled our silence with, "I've been out in the parking lot. Clever parking position there Kyler. I might have missed the dent if I hadn't gone around to the passenger side."

Kyler and I started talking at the same time, trying to apologize.

Eliot interrupted our babbling. "Stop. I'm getting from this the fact that Jamie was driving at the time, and somehow taking instruction from Kyler, right?"

"Yes, sir." He didn't have to say there would be some sort of punishment. Of course, he'd have to tell Michael, who had the final authority over me. While I officially belonged to Michael, I submitted to Eliot, who was, to give it a label, the beta-dom in the household.

"You both seem unhurt."

We nodded and he continued, "Good. We'll have most of this discussion at the house, where anything that needs to follow that little talk can happen in suitable surroundings. Be there at eight. Hopefully, Michael will be home by then. I'm not very upset about the car. I'm concerned about you being safe. Risky driving is clearly a violation of our trust that you'd take care of yourself. The one thing I need clarified now is if this was your fault."

He intended the question for me, but Kyler and I both mumbled, "Yes, sir."

"That's going to complicate things."

***

As I drove us to the apartment, I thought about how most of the time, the confluence of my masochism and my doms' sadism would ultimately pleasure all of us. Not so in the case of a real punishment. Disappointing them with my stupid behavior was already punishment to me, but they'd add something much more tangible. There was also the option to, essentially, safeword out of this. I'd offer to pay for the damage and do some extra work to make up for the trouble. That, however, would make everyone unhappy since we all valued our BDSM hierarchy, both the pleasures and not-so pleasant consequences of the lifestyle. I flashed back to a discussion with Michael several months earlier, when we were defining concepts related to my submission.

I had said to Michael, "A lot of my fantasies are about punishment, but I don't really want something I don't like. It's confusing."

Michael described his definitions, ending with, "Unlike various types of play punishment, real punishment isn't for casual play. That's a special feature of our kind of relationship that I value greatly. Not that I want to do it, but that you'd let me and even want me to. It would probably take a different form, something other than beating you, since I wouldn't want to confuse punishment and reward."

"Makes sense, thanks". After a pause I added, "You haven't had to punish me for real."

"Not yet."

I felt a twinge of excitement at his ominous tone. "What sort of thing would earn that?"

"Dishonesty, depending on the form it takes, probably. Doing something reckless than endangers you or someone else would be a sure way to get in real trouble. I don't think I have to give you a list. It's common-sense stuff…

Lost in thought, my ringing phone startled me and fell under the seat with my fumbling grab. Kyler suggested I focus on driving while he retrieved the phone and checked the number.

"Says 'Master Michael.' Aren't you afraid people will see that?"

"Please tell him I'm driving. And no."

Kyler did and his only other words into the phone were, "Yes, sir. I will, sir." He tucked the phone into my pocket. "He was pleased to hear you were, quote, 'so concerned about safe driving'. It's good to know he has a sense of humor. You're supposed to call him when you get to the apartment."

***

"What did Michael say?"

"Not much, except he's disappointed, and that I should do whatever Eliot tells me. He was busy with whatever was keeping him at work."

"I got you into this and I'm going ask Eliot to punish me too. It's only fair."

I stared, not trying to hide my shock. Kyler's interest in the scene was usually limited to voyeur at Michael and Eliot's parties and some private experimentation with me or the three of us. "You don't have to do that. I was the driver, and I made the choice."

"Still, I think I pressured you, so I owe Eliot something."

I wasn't sure how to reply, partly because I agreed. "Are you sure?"

"Yes. I want to show him I'm serious about taking responsibility. And don't you think it would make us closer? I'd have a better idea of what you go through."

Wow. "I hadn't thought of that. I've been concerned about saving your butt."

"Thanks. And what about yours? What's he going to do?"

"No clue. They've never given me a serious punishment before, and since I usually like being beaten, he'd have to come up with something else."

***

All too soon, we found ourselves in Eliot's living room, reviewing what happened.

"Jamie, you put me in the uncomfortable position of having to punish you. Although you know how much I love that little car, you're in trouble because you could have been seriously hurt, or worse. I talked to Michael, who's still stuck at work, and he's fine with me handling this as I see fit." With a heavy sigh and a tone bordering on annoyance, Eliot said, "Kyler, why are you here?"

"Because it's partly my fault, and I should be punished if he is."

"You're not my submissive, nor anyone else's as far as I know."

"I don't mean to argue, sir, but I talked Jamie into this and got him in trouble. I'm willing to stand by him now."

"I'd say you helped Jamie get himself in trouble. I appreciate the gesture. If you're serious, I'll include you, but there's no backing out. I'm in no mood for nonsense."

"I understand. I'm serious."

"Fine. I'll be back in a few minutes." Eliot headed for the kitchen. "Wait there." After what seemed like a long time, he yelled into the living room, "I'll be another few minutes."

"What do you think he's doing in there?" Kyler whispered to me. "Aren't the implements of our destruction in the basement?"

"You'd be surprised."

"Great. He's not going to use hot peppers on our dicks, is he?"

"Where'd you get that crazy idea?"

"From that blog you showed me."

"Hardly anyone does that for real." I was guessing that Eliot needed some time to figure out Kyler's punishment.

Eliot eventually returned and announced, "Here's the situation. Ky, I'm sure you know that the traditional punishment is some sort of spanking or whipping. That'll work fine for you. Jamie, you know that if I whipped you hard enough to make it a real punishment, you'd be damaged more than I'm willing to do and I don't have a physical alternative in mind. You're coming with me now. Ky, you can use my office to wait. Feel free to surf the net."

I followed Eliot's purposeful stride to the dungeon. Once there and having received no other instructions, I watched him peruse the contents of a cabinet holding various impact implements. As he fingered the items he said, "*You* will administer Kyler's punishment."

Me? "Oh no... no, sir, I can't do that. He's my best friend. Besides, I don't know how."

"I am *not* giving you a choice of the punishment you've consented to. It's punishment, something you don't like. By definition. As for technique, I'll show you."

"Please don't make me do this, sir."

"I'm open to suggestions." Eliot folded his arms over his chest and watched me expectantly.

Jamie to brain... something... anything... fuck. "I... I guess don't have any."

"Stand by the cross." Eliot indicated the wooden St. Andrew's cross, a place of delights up to this moment. "Get the lights first. All the way up."

Whatever he had in mind apparently needed better visibility than our regular scene ambience. That didn't tell me much.

Eliot held a small, five-tailed cat he hadn't used on me before. The strands were made of rubber cords folded in half and twisted the entire length, leaving a loop at the striking end. While it might not look wicked, I knew our other rubber cat hurt a lot more than similar toys made of leather. I mean, it hurt in a good way, leaving awesome marks. "My friend, who makes these, calls it the Johnny Corkscrew. Easy to use, no real skill needed." He shoved the cat into my hand and picked up a colorful striped pillow that he tied to the middle of the bondage cross. At my puzzled expression he explained, "Your practice victim is the pillow. The stripes allow you to pick a target and see where the lashes land."

It was remarkably easy to aim. Unfortunately, that was the least of my concerns. I tried to forget about the target I'd be facing. When Eliot had me try it from the other side of the cross, I saw Michael in the doorway. *How long had he been watching? Did Eliot know he was there?* Eliot answered my second question.

"Hey hon, glad to see you. More than you know."

"I have an idea," Michael replied. "Kyler said you two have been down here a while, but I don't see anything terrible going on. The bottle of Jack in the kitchen had me wondering."

Without thinking, I wailed, "He's making me beat Kyler as my punishment!"

"How creative." Michael took a small object out of his pocket and asked me, "Aren't you forgetting something?"

Shit. I wasn't allowed to speak to Michael until my collar was locked on. I always wear a stainless steel chain that looks like regular jewelry but has links large enough to accept the small padlock Michael attaches when I'm with him. My first words after it was locked in place were an apology, which he accepted.

"Eliot?"

Eliot gave him an overview. "While we're certain the pillow won't dare misbehave again, he's concerned about doing something wrong with his best friend on the cross."

"I like your plan, but we need to give him a more realistic target. I volunteer." Michael started removing his trousers and I was certain my panic was obvious to them. "Don't worry, I can handle this," Michael said.

"But you're not supposed to bottom to me!"

"Boy, I'm not bottoming. I'm a teaching tool. *You* are obeying Eliot's instructions, and mine too, by the way. You need to see how your strokes appear on flesh."

Michael didn't wait for my agreement as he positioned himself on the cross. I froze.

"Do it, boy."

After a lot of prompting with a weird mix of threat and encouragement, I managed to land some competent strokes across Michael's ass. Although I knew he was no stranger to the business end of a whip, his quiet acceptance of my novice efforts surprised me. He did nothing except say "good one" a few times, and "harder" more than a few.

After they deemed me adequately trained, Eliot asked Michael to send Kyler down. "But first, do you want to add anything?"

"Actually, yes. Jamie, I hesitate to do this because I'll have to suffer too, but I'm not going to take you to Justin's party Saturday. He invited you and I won't

SCANDALOUS

forbid you to go on your own. Let me know if you decide to go."

That was worse than having to beat Kyler. In what I hoped was a steady voice I said, "I'll let you know before Saturday." I didn't like the idea of going on my own, but Justin and Toby gave great parties. I must have looked like I needed a hug because Michael held out an arm. I took a step closer, and Michael pulled me in. "I'm sorry, sir," I said into his chest.

"So am I. That was a pretty boneheaded thing to do, you know."

"Yes, sir. Thank you for punishing me."

***

Kyler walked in and looked around. He'd been here a few times before, so the confusion on his face must have come from the absence of any punishment activity.

"Over here," Eliot ordered. "Get undressed." He then led Kyler to the cross, guiding him flat against it, facing the wall. "Arms up." Eliot attached his wrists to the restraints on each side and blindfolded him. Eliot announced, with irritating jocularity, "I have good news and bad news." He paused for effect. "The good news is that I'm not going to beat you."

Kyler tensed. He was on the cross and had been more or less told he'd be beaten.

"The bad news, more so for Jamie, I think, is that Jamie is going to do it. Since you managed to get in trouble together, it seems fitting that you are punished simultaneously. You'll get approximately thirty lashes, though the number could change with Jamie's performance. If he doesn't deliver the required strokes properly, they'll be repeated. If for some reason he stops, I'll take over, but the remaining strokes will double in number. I've instructed him to not go easy on you. Any questions?"

"Am I allowed to talk or make noise, and do I have to count?"

"No counting. Make any noise you want, but don't ask for anything unless there's a real physical problem, like your arms getting numb."

"Got it, sir."

Eliot stepped away and motioned for me to get into position. I started, "What do I..." but Eliot put up a hand.

"I'll give complete instructions as to the when and where. You need only be concerned with obeying. Start with a total of ten here," pointing at Kyler's lovely pale ass, "changing sides every two or three."

My first stroke was fairly weak. *Fuck, this is much more difficult than I thought.* Eliot caught my arm as I raised it for the next stroke.

"The first one didn't count. You were much better before. Don't keep us here all night."

"I'll do better, sir."

I managed to complete that set and the next without needing correction. I hesitated briefly the few times Kyler yelped or grunted, partly out of concern, but also because it was, disconcertingly, arousing. How could I not react to a fine ass, currently naked, with bright red twisted marks made by that evil little toy? He didn't make much noise, but it had to hurt, and I wondered if his apparent stoicism was for my benefit.

At twenty, Eliot repositioned Kyler to face out, which somehow seemed worse, like he was watching me, making me feel more guilty for hurting him, not to mention my getting hard. Silly, I knew, since he was still blindfolded, but the pause in the action reset my brain. "*Please*, sir, don't make me do this."

"You know the rules, Jamie; if I take over, it's twenty more. They might be a bit harder as well."

"Noooo... I don't want Kyler to get extra."

"Then continue."

Kyler spoke up. "It's okay, you can stop, and I'll take the extra."

It didn't sound like he meant that, which didn't matter since there was no way I'd subject him to more. What it did was snap me out of my anguish. "No! I mean, thank you, but I can't let you do that. I'll finish."

After I delivered a few lashes to Kyler's chest, Eliot said, "You're doing well. Only six more to go. This is your next target," pointing at the top of Kyler's thighs. "Three each."

That was too close to some of Kyler's most vulnerable, not to mention favorite, parts. "What if I miss?"

"You've been doing fine."

I hesitated, and said, "I'll do it, but, please, sir, couldn't we protect him somehow?"

Eliot arranged a towel over Kyler's groin and held it in place. "No more delays. Do it."

I did as instructed, and tossed the cat away.

"Pick it up. You know how to treat toys." While I silently complied, Eliot released Kyler and gave him a gentle hug. "You okay?"

Kyler nodded. "You did well for what I assume was your first flogging."

Eliot motioned for me to join the hug.

"Thank you for punishing me, sir." I couldn't look at Kyler, who apparently saw my distress anyway.

Kyler said, "Don't be upset. You were only doing what you had to. Have to admit, though, I'm even less clear about why you like this. And why did you thank Eliot?"

"Hard to explain."

"Jamie, if I may?" Eliot offered.

I nodded.

"Jamie, would you have preferred not being punished?"

"No, sir."

"Would you say I made considerable effort to do something I didn't like in order to give you something you needed or wanted?"

"Yes, sir."

"Would you say you appreciate having the opportunity to submit to Michael and me?"

"Yes, sir."

"Kyler, does that help?"

"Yeah, I think I get it. I should thank you, too."

"You can thank me by not doing anything like that again."

When Kyler reached for his clothes, Eliot suggested he would be more comfortable wearing the towel. "You two can use the guest bedroom."

Upstairs, as I carefully rubbed soothing lotion over Kyler's marks. I tried not to focus on how erotic I found his warm, slightly ridged skin. I said, "I'm so sorry. I didn't want to do this."

"Stop worrying about it. It's over."

"There's something else bothering me, but I'm not sure I want to talk about it."

"You know you can tell me anything."

"I was getting hard when I was beating you. I feel awful."

Kyler sat up, so quickly he knocked over the lotion, and almost tipped me off the bed. He gave me a big hug and said, "Not a problem! I think the little head was just responding to my naked, whipped body. What's not to like, kinky boy? Do you think you actually enjoyed it?"

"I'm pretty sure that at least ninety percent of me hated it. I'm just not sure about the rest."

"There's not a big percentage left. Maybe you were subconsciously thinking of having our roles reversed."

"You know just what to say. Thanks. I still feel like crap."

Kyler frowned. "This isn't fair. You're not likely to forget as quickly as I can heal. How can I help?"

"Well, you could spank me or something. I'd feel *so* much better if I had something physical to focus on."

"If you're sure." Kyler went to the door. "I'll be right back." He returned with the Johnny Corkscrew and a promise to tell me everything Eliot said when he asked to borrow it.

It took some prompting, but not much, to convince Kyler to put some arm behind the strokes. I made a mental note to ask later why he seemed comfortable doing it – both the technical aspect and apparent willingness. I was fairly certain he didn't go around whipping people.

I relaxed into the familiar rush of pain, and the pleasure from the intimacy of the act. This time, I welcomed my swelling cock and hoped Kyler wasn't too sore to play a bit. Invigorated by a warmed, tingling ass and a forgiving friend, I offered to suck his rising cock.

"Try lying on your side. That doesn't hurt, right?"

After a leisurely exchange of blow jobs, I gathered Kyler in my arms, much like when the day had started, a seemingly long time ago.

SCANDALEUSE

Colton Aalto

Exhaling in relief, I dropped into my desk chair as the last fifth grader exited my classroom. Teachers routinely describe the last day of school before spring break as a day from hell, and today the characterization was spot-on. My kids were ready for a break, overly excited about their coming vacations and totally unfocussed on schoolwork. On top of that, I had gone head-to-head with Buzz Ingraham, the school's resident bully, not once but twice. My blood boiled whenever I caught him harassing and belittling other kids, and since the beginning of school, I'd been on a mission to reign him in. The problem would have solved itself long ago if his mother hadn't taken his side repeatedly, convinced every kid was picking on him, every adult was biased against him, and her baby couldn't be wrong. Facts didn't register with her.

With the school day over, the other teachers quickly dispersed while I collected papers to grade over the break. The building was almost empty when I climbed into my cycling clothes; I biked the fifteen miles from my apartment whenever the weather permitted. But, as I retrieved my bicycle, Ella Summer, the school's secretary, appeared. Her pursed lips and dour expression signaled that she wasn't bringing good news.

I sighed as she handed me a letter. "Mrs. Ingraham complaining again?"

She gritted her teeth. "Much worse, although that witch's fingerprints are all over this."

Ella didn't like Buzz's mother in the least, but it wasn't like her to call anyone a witch. I was surprised she was so upset, although she was my biggest defender at the school. She'd liked me from the start, perhaps because I treated her as an equal, and occasionally brought her flowers or other small gifts, because I knew how thankless her job was and how much shit she took. When word leaked out that I was gay, she doubled down in support of me, partly because her son was gay, too.

Scanning the letter, I frowned in disbelief. The head of the school board was summarily announcing I'd been fired, effective immediately. "What's this all about? Is it a joke?"

Ella shook her head. "It's those videos. Lord only knows why she was patrolling the internet for gay male movies."

"*What*??" None of that made any sense. My firing had to be a mistake. But before I could press her for details, my cell rang. Tempted to ignore it, I relented when I saw it was my mom, calling from work. Because my grandmother was fighting cancer and not doing well, every time she called for the last couple of weeks,

I worried it was about an emergency. Ella slipped away as I answered.

"Zac, your aunt wants to talk to you. Can you drop by on your way home?"

Still reeling from being fired, I protested. "Uh, Mom, this isn't a good time."

"Zac, that woman is a saint and has done a ton for you. You can take five minutes to see her." I sighed, accepting the inevitable.

My Aunt Bea—short for Beatrice—had been a second parent to me, filling the hole in my life left by the absence of my father, who I'd never met. Thirteen years ago, she and Mom returned from a short vacation to California and broke the news that they'd taken the trip to get married. Aunt Bea, who technically wasn't my aunt, was now my second mother. We just never bothered to change what I called her. For me, their marriage merely formalized what I guess I always knew about them. I was mostly pissed that they hadn't taken me to California. Hey, I was only ten....

When I arrived, Bea was in full crisis mode. She was always the strong one, in control and clear-headed in emergencies.

"We need to talk about the movies that they used as an excuse to fire you."

Movies again; what the hell? "*What movies*?? Wait... you know I got fired??"

"Oh, it's all over social media. Scandal of the year in this town. Mrs. Ingraham made sure of that. As for the gay porn movies... The young man in them is your father." I blinked in disbelief, struggling to wrap my head around what she'd said.

I was in a fog as she explained that my father filmed a dozen gay porn movies when he was 21. He'd done it to raise cash to help my mother, after she got pregnant. Apparently, my lesbian mother and gay father decided to experiment and slept together: exactly once. Once was all it took. Before I was born, my father and the producer of his porn films died in a car crash, on the way home from a dinner where they had been discussing their next project. My father left behind little other than unseen work in gay porn. The producer's heirs weren't interested in entering the world of pornography, but a few days ago, someone got access to the forgotten films and began selling them on the internet.

People jumped to the conclusion that I was the movies' star because, as well as something of a family resemblance, my father and I shared a massive, distinctive tattoo – an elaborate dragon whose head was perched on my shoulder, whose tail curled across my chest and whose mouth shot flames up to my ear. I'd gotten it years ago in a burst of youthful angst and rebellion, as a sign of solidarity with a man I'd never met. At 23 I was more muscular than my father had been so, except for the tattoo, we wouldn't have been confused, or at least there would have been a good chance of people believing the similarity was pure chance. But Mrs. Ingraham and her right-wing allies on the school board ignored that and treated the tat as a smoking gun. They'd been looking for an excuse to go after me ever since word leaked out that I was gay.

Bea finished by telling me she'd talked to a lawyer and hired an investigator to authenticate the age of the films. My record would be cleared, but not before the end of the school year. I was looking at an extra two months of summer vacation.

I biked home in a daze.

The scandal consumed the city for the next week. Just when the story might have run out of steam, the right-wing media picked it up, responding to Mrs. Ingraham's gloating posts on social media. Eager to stoke the culture wars, they played up the perceived horror of a gay porn actor being around fifth graders, spicing the story with invented rumors from unnamed—of course—sources claiming I routinely had sex at school. The veiled suggestion was that kids might be involved. The left-wing media, monitoring the nutcases on the right, got wind of the story and reacted predictably, bemoaning the outrage of a teacher—a dedicated one who was the best in the school, by all accounts—being fired merely for being gay. The school's teachers and virtually all of my kids' parents rallied around me as the community split into warring camps. The media scrutiny was intense and endless.

Exhausted by the tumult, I hauled myself to school to clean out my room on the last day of spring break, a week after being fired. More than anything, I'd miss the kids, but I was partly relieved to be out of a job so I could get away for a while. Of course, being freshly unemployed, the places I could visit weren't garden spots, so instead I'd likely hole up in my apartment for the duration, escaping only for long bicycle rides.

I was surprised when a tall, handsome Black man met me at school. He was close to my age and while we hadn't met, I recognized him as Ella's son, Addis.

He spotted me and a smile broke over his face, making him more handsome than I thought possible.

He extended his hand. "Addis Summer. Happened to be visiting Mom and she told me to get my ass over here and help you clean out your room. She thought my presence might help deter trouble."

I managed only a mumbled, "Um, thanks." Ella had been trying to set me up with him ever since the news broke that I was gay. He was a high-profile model and the pictures she showed me piqued my curiosity to the point that I spent an inordinately long time checking out his social media and ogling the stunning photos of him on the internet. The man was even more impressive in person, and seeing him made me regret that I hadn't acted on her numerous overtures. Of course, even with her pushing things, it wasn't like I'd have a chance with a famous model like him.

"You know, she's a big fan of yours. She told me so much about you that I feel like we grew up together. She keeps pestering me to hit you up."

"Yeah, she suggested the same to me."

"Well, after we clean out your room, I'll buy you a drink. That way I can tell her I made a pass at you." He winked and gave me a conspiratorial grin, making my heart flutter a bit.

We set about boxing up stuff and, once done, I left the papers I graded over break and the detailed lesson plans I wrote for whoever would take my place. Through it all, Addis was engaging and interesting. I felt like I already knew him from reading his social media posts but talking to him in person cemented my favorable image of him. It was obvious he was gorgeous, but he was also open and friendly, with a great sense of humor. Being around him was comfortable. I joked that to make Ella happy we should claim the afternoon in my classroom was a date, and I got a warm feeling when he grinned and said it was better than a date because we'd gotten to know each other so well.

As it came time to leave, he got a devilish look on his face. "I like your idea of treating this as a date, Zac. Since we're both gay, we're used to sleeping with men on the first date, so… just sayin'." I felt my face turn red, wondering if he thought I was easy. Yeah, I'd slept with a man on the first date, but I'd never made it a habit.

"You're cute when you blush. Not something I see from Black men or women. But I digress. If we want to claim this is a first date, I say we go all the way and fuck." He pulled me close and wrapped his arms around me.

Damn, the man was serious about hooking up! I was stunned by his forwardness.

"C'mon, Zac, let your hair down and live a little."

Things were happening too fast, but I wanted him, and probably wouldn't get another chance. It might seem tawdry to get in on with a dude you'd only met a few hours earlier, but….

I took a deep breath. "Where do you want to go?"

"What's wrong with right here?"

"*Here??*"

"Yeah. In my last year of high school I had a huge crush on a teacher and fantasized that one day he'd bend me over his desk when nobody was around. Time to turn fantasy into reality. Nobody is in the building, and even if somebody were, what's the worst that can happen? They fire you? Oh, wait, they already did that.

113

They believe you've had sex inside these four walls anyway; let's give them something to gossip about." He leaned forward and pressed his thick, soft lips against mine. They felt amazing and I opened my mouth. Kissing the stud was heavenly.

Addis obviously had a reckless streak. I did too on occasion. Mine surfaced as the tension from the crazy week suddenly broke. "So, in your fantasy with the teacher, are you naked when he bends you over his desk?"

"Oh yeah," he deadpanned. "Not a stitch of clothing on me." I began unbuttoning his shirt.

An hour later, I turned out the lights in my classroom for the final time, thinking it might be good that I wouldn't be returning anytime soon. The vision of Addis on my desk was seared in my memory, and every time I entered the room my mind would wander back to what we'd done on it. As bad as the week had been, I was suddenly on an incredible high.

Leaving the building, I began feeling guilty. If he thought I was easy before, now he must be convinced of it. "Look, about what we just did… I'm not really like that. I mean, I slept with a man after a first date once, but having sex in my classroom with someone I've barely met…"

"*Really?*" His voice dripped skepticism.

"No, really! I mean, I've never done anything like that. It's just after the last week… well, I've been out of myself."

"Well, I'm glad to know what I'm up against. Because that was the hottest damn sex I can remember, and if you think you can get rid of me with a 'thank you ma'am' after the wham bam, you're mistaken."

"It's not like that!" I paused. "You aren't, you know, put off by what happened?"

"Hell no. I initiated things, if you recall. Despite what *you* may think, it's not my style to hit on dudes I've just met, but I'm learning to grab opportunities when they arise. Relax! Even though I've already taken advantage of you, I'll still buy you that drink."

"Well, I can't apply for unemployment benefits until Monday, so I'm free."

He laughed. "Let's get dinner after drinks. I have a proposition for you."

"I thought I'd already been propositioned."

He chuckled. "Yup. But this is about a job. We'll discuss it later."

Over dinner, I couldn't stop staring into his dark eyes. He was charming, not to mention sexy as hell. As we finished, he leaned over the table. "About the proposition. Mom probably told you I do some modeling. I have a great, creative agent and she's constantly in touch with the major advertising agencies. One has a project for a high-end French perfume line, *Scandaleuse* – the feminine version of scandalous for the French-challenged. They're launching a big advertising campaign and when she heard about your situation with the porn videos, something clicked.

"The face of *Scandaleuse* is a beautiful, famous French actress. My agent's idea is to pair us with her. The French, after all, are the masters of the *ménage à trois*. The campaign will be elegant, suggestive of breaking taboos and hinting of scandalous behavior; you and I will add the taint of scandal to her impeccable reputation. You know, older woman with

115

a much younger man. Older woman with *two* younger men. Two women staring at each other suggestively while frustrated men look on helplessly. White woman with a Black man, although that's cliche. White woman of means dominating a tatted, bad boy. *That* I want to see. Two gorgeous women wrapped in each other's arms as two men stand at attention, waiting to serve them. Beautiful woman dipping her feet in a spectacular swimming pool while two skinny-dipping boys stare into each other's eyes. Two handsome young men in tuxedos escorting a scantily clad woman into an elegant dining club. Two women torturing a young man in bondage. A stunningly beautiful woman behind a lavish mask being escorted to Venice's Carnevale by two masked men clad only in sequined jock straps. The possibilities are luscious, not to mention endless. Plus, there will be tongue-in-cheek opportunities to include reminders of our real-life scandals. We've both been swept up in them."

My head was spinning. The idea was preposterous, starting with the inconvenient fact that I was nothing more than a fifth-grade teacher. "Uh, hello, I'm just a guy. I teach fifth graders. I'm not a model."

"Not yet. But my agent has seen enough photos that she's ready to sign you."

"What photos?"

"*Duh*. The porn videos. But beyond those, we live in an era of social media. Your 15 minutes of fame—okay, maybe a week of fame by now—caused the paparazzi and the media to unearth a trove of photos. Most from your college days, most shirtless, and most hot. Diving team photos, in tiny Speedos no less, but you apparently had a boyfriend who was quite a shutterbug and a fan of putting you into erotic poses.

116

If you haven't searched the internet in the last week, you should. Your bare skin is *everywhere*. Mom had some recent pictures of you in your cycling clothes and from a wet T-shirt fundraiser that confirmed you're still in shape. After what I saw this afternoon, you might be in better shape than ever. I work with models all the time, and trust me, you've got what it takes." He licked his lips and gave me a suggestive look.

If my lack of modeling experience wouldn't kill the deal, the mistake about my father's porn videos would. Taking a deep breath, I explained that I wasn't the porn star, and ergo, didn't add a real scandal to the mix. Addis frowned as I talked, then laughed. "Scandals are easy to launch, impossible to put back in the bottle. *The New York Times* could print a front-page story about how you aren't the boy in the movies and two thirds of the country will still believe you were. Besides, when your story came out, my agent said that there's no such thing as bad publicity.

"But aside from that... Did I mention that we'd be on Ibiza for a month during filming? The advertising agency will rent a villa that we'd be able to enjoy when we weren't in front of the cameras. Nice pool, spectacular views, or spectacular pool, awesome views? Whatever. A real love nest. We might be able to extend the stay if my agent unearths more modelling opportunities. Advertising agencies love summer in the Mediterranean, and they love Ibiza in particular."

A month in Ibiza with Addis sounded too good to be true, but his question brought to the surface an issue I'd struggled with. If the truth about my father being in the porn videos came out in an effort to restore my wholesome image, the spotlight would be on the awkward story of him and my mother, not to mention Mom and Bea. Bea wouldn't be phased, but Mom was different. I didn't want to put her through that. Addis was right; it wasn't like clearing my name would salvage my reputation anyway. The damage was done.

Clearing my name wouldn't get my old teaching job back before the end of the school year, and I'd already decided to move on. I student-taught at an inner-city school and found it much more rewarding than the affluent school where I'd spent the year. The inner-city school's principal had seen the news about my firing and already told me she had a job for me, and I'd be welcomed with open arms. More than welcomed; even though I'd only student-taught, some kids and parents were still asking about me.

I needed time to think. For a diversion I asked about Addis's scandal.

"Ah, well, despite what you might think after this afternoon, mine doesn't involve the teacher I had a crush on. But I was wild in my younger days and, to make a long story short, a famous televangelist hired me for... well, you know what. I was up for whatever, he had a plantation fetish, and I had the black skin to make it happen. For a 22-year-old, money to burn and travel to exotic places was a no-brainer.

"Things went fine until we were spotted on an airplane. He doubled down, making up an idiotic story about hiring me for his wife and claiming it was only to help a poor boy from the ghetto. His story unraveled when it came out that he'd filmed me and shared the films with members of a shady group, one of whom got nervous and spilled the beans. Big, big scandal. They got him on tax evasion – I kid you not, the fool deducted what he paid me as charitable contributions, claiming he was helping poor Black boys from the ghetto." He paused and gave me a grin. "Maybe we can photoshop your dad's films with mine, so it looks like the two of us are having a gay old time. Sex tapes are the gold standard of publicity. The gift that never stops giving."

Addis insisted on picking up the check, saying he'd never permit an unemployed man to pay and besides, his mother would be mad unless he did. I excused myself to go to the restroom and on the way back glanced at my text. I had an urgent message from Bea, warning me that right-wing nuts were picketing my apartment building; they apparently weren't satisfied with merely getting me fired and were seeking God knows what else. They'd been set off by some of the photos my boyfriend took in college. I knew those would come back to haunt me when he took them, but 19-year-olds aren't known for fully considering the consequences of things they do. She suggested I spend the night somewhere else to avoid confrontations. She and Mom were hosting a couple of friends, so sleeping on their floor wasn't a great option.

How much more could the situation escalate? Getting away to Ibiza was sounding better and better.

Addis was signing the credit card receipt as I returned. I sat down and said dryly, "Apparently I'm not only unemployed but homeless, too."

When I explained, he grinned. "That's great! My agent will be thrilled by the extra publicity. That also means I get to aid the homeless tonight. Are you up for an encore or two of what we did in the schoolroom? I have a stack of fantasies that involve hot men, and most don't even require a teacher's desk. Mom will be thrilled to fix you breakfast tomorrow morning. I mean, she'll be thrilled beyond belief."

After what I'd been through, the thought of spending the night in Addis's arms and waking to Ella's breakfast sounded heavenly. I gratefully accepted, feeling excited. I'd also have time to think through his modeling proposal.

Hell, what was there to think about? What gay boy in his right mind would turn down a month in Ibiza with a gorgeous model who was charming and interesting? The scandal could play out on its own, with the identity of the porn star remaining a secret. My dad was gone before he could give me anything other than his genes, but ironically the one thing he'd done to help me had opened a door decades later.

"So, how soon can your agent get me a contract? For Ibiza."

"Done. I had her send it while you were in the restroom." Addis scrolled to a formal document on his cell. "Here. You can sign digitally. Make sure your passport is current because we can be on a flight first thing Monday."

Everyone can use a scandal in their life, even if it's not their own doing...

TWINKLETOES

Zak Jane Keir

It was mid-morning and Miss Juliet was sitting at her desk, in the upstairs office, scrolling through her emails. Valley Chateau's social media was at least partly automated, and she could rely on her boys to deal with some of it themselves, even now, from their own homes, but the emails were a constant. There were multiple accounts to deal with: one for notifications that any film clips or Valley Chateau merchandise had sold; another for aspiring performers and a third for event enquiries: she had now managed to set automatic shutdown-due-to-lockdown replies to the latter two. But there were personal client bookings to address, which needed personal replies, general admin and then all the rest. Spammers seemed to have got more creative when it came to bypassing the filters, these days. She didn't need SEO optimisation, nor to invest in Bitcoin; she certainly didn't want affordable cosmetic surgery. She might not be 25 anymore but, as she'd been told many times, she had good bone structure, and she was quite comfortable with looking 'mature'. Being fair-haired meant that going grey was no big deal, either.

She was about two-thirds of the way through her inbox when she spotted a subject header HEY TWINKLETOES and paused. There was really only one person who would address her that way: even bratty subs tended to be a little more respectful in an initial approach. She'd told him often enough that she would always read an email from him because she knew his email address, but it was a habit she hadn't been able to break him of. With a slightly reluctant smile, she opened the message.

Hey Twinkletoes!

Doing a piece on how porn stars and so on are dealing with everything during the pandemic. Want in on it? Yes I know you will probably say No but might as well ask. Video chat at a time that suits you. And hope you're coping, anyway. Usual guarantee that nothing will be published without your permission but strange times and all that, thought I'd get in touch.

F

Miss Juliet contemplated. She could simply refuse; of course she could. It wasn't as if Valley Chateau needed any scrap of attention going. Yes, there was always the possibility that getting another namecheck in mainstream media would bring new clients, but would it bring in more clients, or just more pests? People had more time on their hands at present and while that meant some of them had the leisure and inclination to explore their sexualities, it also meant that busybodies, concern trolls and utter wingnuts had little to do other than leap up and down, screeching their outrage on every available platform. She had been operating for more than 20 years by now, neither

122

particularly courting publicity nor running away from it, but remaining ready to adapt. Miss Juliet, once plain old Julie Heath from Mitcham, had always been good at adapting, though she was well aware some of her success was due to luck. Luck, and Oliver. And, quite possibly, Frank himself.

Of all those who had approached her for an interview back then, Frank had been the only one to ask how she was coping in a way that seemed genuine, so he had been the only one she agreed to talk to. Over the years, they had both become increasingly successful and, despite their very different fields of expertise, they had never wholly lost touch. Miss Juliet of Valley Chateau remained the almost-respectable face of femdom and the BDSM lifestyle, while *So Frank*, once a column that had moved from magazine to national newspaper and finally to one of the most popular video channels outside of beauty, wellness and computer games, had somehow retained its status as trustworthy, even these days. Perhaps some of his trustworthiness was down to Miss Juliet, and the things that had happened between them. And perhaps her instincts regarding who to trust had been influenced by their first encounter, as well.

She hadn't been flying under the radar then, of course. She had been in the centre of the storm, those few terrible weeks. Doorstepped in her dressing gown, chased down the street when she went to shop for food, written about in all sorts of snarky terms: slut, whore, pervert, gold-digger and the rest of it. At least one newspaper had called her a witch, which had given her one little moment of rueful amusement. Witch? Really?

Miss Juliet got up and began to pace. The sunlight was pouring in through the windows, and the garden, not too overgrown as yet, looked enticing. It was such a horribly beautiful spring this year, when everyone was being ordered not to enjoy it: stay home, stay at home, stay in your cage. She remembered it being a beautiful spring when Oliver died.

He'd been the twenty-seventh-richest man in England, or so he had told her, quite early on. She hadn't entirely believed him, but she hadn't been all that bothered, at first. She liked him, and she loved dominating him, and he loved submitting to her. She hadn't been doing it professionally for all that long when they met, though she had been starting to think it was a better career option than book-keeping.

He came to see her a lot, and the point where the border between client and friend began to blur happened fairly quickly. He never wanted her to stop seeing clients; he found it exciting, and she enjoyed the fact that he enjoyed it. From the start, he'd liked to buy her things, expensive things, way above what she'd been used to asking for. He'd also begun to encourage her to think ahead, think big, or at least bigger. He had the money to rent hotel suites and even private members' clubs, for exclusive little parties, and some less little ones. He had talked about bankrolling a film company for high-class, artistic productions: Juliet had liked the idea but believed it to be more of a fantasy than a serious proposition.

It all had to be discreet, of course. In the 1990s, any indication that you might be kinky meant huge scandal, ruination, mockery by the press, public dismissal and all the rest of it, especially for someone as high profile as Oliver. He had begun to tell her that he didn't care, that it didn't matter. He had begun to talk about marriage. Then came the accident.

Miss Juliet shook her head and made for the kitchen. What she needed now was tea: a whole pot of Earl Grey. It wasn't accurate to say that she hadn't thought about Oliver in years; she thought of him often, with a degree of fondness and a little curiosity as to what he would make of the direction her life had taken. What had come back to her now, though, with startling force, was his death and the immediate aftermath.

She had been devastated, and the grief had taken her by surprise. While she had suspected that Oliver might love her, she never considered that what she felt for him was anything more than an appreciation of kinks that matched hers, pleasure in his company and a degree of gratitude.

She'd found out via a news bulletin on the radio: she wasn't 'family', she had no official status, so the police hadn't come to break the news to her. The verdict at the inquest was that he had probably swerved to avoid an animal in the road, which at least fitted with the Oliver Juliet had known, but his playbag had been in the boot of the car: his collar, his favourite dildo, his leather chaps, along with several copies of Juliet's most recent business card, because he had taken the photo she was using. And, of course, the last call he'd made on his mobile had been to her. It wasn't long before someone passed the details onto the press.

Maybe Frank had come along at the right time, when she was ready to talk to someone but, Juliet, ever after, suspected that choosing him had been the best decision for both of them.

"Just putting my foot in the door, well, not jamming it in the door, if you get my drift," he had written. "It must be tough, are you coping OK? I'd like to do a story on you if you want to talk, and I'm not an arsehole, at least not as much of an arsehole as a lot of the others." The letter was posted, not scrawled on a sheet torn out of a notebook and shoved through the letterbox. It was on nice stationery. She'd phoned the number he gave, telling herself she could just hang up if she detected arseholery.

Juliet drank her tea at the kitchen table, sitting on the hard, wooden chair nearest the cooker. The kitchen was untidy, much untidier than it would normally be, or so she supposed: She had, for years, been accustomed to leaving kitchen duties to whichever subby boys were in residence at any given time. But now she was alone, entirely alone, and therefore cooking and cleaning were either done by her or left undone.

She'd still been living in her Holborn flat when Oliver died, and she'd been alone then. She remembered forcing herself to tidy and clean it once she'd agreed to allow this Frank person to interview her. She never saw clients in the flat so the front room was unremarkably furnished, apart from the Mapplethorpe and Giger prints on the walls, and the bookcase being full of erotica.

He arrived one minute before the time they'd agreed, which she thought reasonable enough. She had spent some time fretting about what to wear and decided, eventually, on her holly-green button-fronted dress: one of the ones she would wear if Oliver wanted to take her out to dinner. It was just low enough to show some cleavage, just short enough to show some thigh, but it wasn't blatantly sexy, and it looked more expensive than it was. To put on leather or latex to talk to a journalist, or to greet him in her dressing gown and slippers, would have been cliched and silly, and she was determined to be neither.

Thinking along those lines made her decide to remain barefoot, as well: she was in her own home and being informal, so no need for heels. She didn't want to put boots on; she thought it might be a while before she could bear to wear her boots again. Oliver had bought her several pairs, and had loved to put them on her and take them off again, making a ritual of it.

Frank was a small, slender man with tinted glasses and light brown hair cut in a 60s-throwback style that didn't really suit him. He had a kind face, and a reassuring manner, even though she suspected he was a year or two younger than she was. She offered tea and he accepted, and they sat in the front room, the sunlight streaming in through the window, routine traffic sounds in the background, making a little small talk.

She noticed he was looking at her bare feet. She stretched them out, wriggled her toes, then drew them back, crossing her ankles. He kept looking, then he noticed that she had noticed. He licked his lips, then took out a notebook and a pen.

"How long had you known Oliver Chippenham?" he asked.

"Quite a while," she said, glad that her voice didn't crack. She could do this, of course she could.

The only picture of Oliver that was on display in Valley Chateau was a painting that had been done from Juliet's favourite photograph, taken at one of the most public fetish events Oliver had ever attended with her. He had been wearing a full bodysuit of black latex, complete with a hood that revealed only his eyes and mouth, and it had been his idea to visit the photographer's portrait booth; Juliet had been mildly concerned that, even hooded, Oliver might be recognised, but as far as she knew, even decades later, no one had ever publicly identified the masked, kneeling foot-worshipper reverently kissing the toes of Miss Juliet, as Oliver Chippenham. Even the artist she commissioned to paint the scene for her hadn't asked her which of her slaves she was choosing to honour with such an artwork.

Juliet, having finished her tea, went to the hall and stood in front of the picture, gazing at it. What would Oliver have made of this current crisis, she wondered. Would he have married her, if he had lived, and would such a marriage have lasted this long? She realised she had no idea.

The interview had been long, but not unacceptably so, and now it appeared to be drawing to a close. Juliet had found it easier than she expected to talk about Oliver and, to an extent, about herself. It might have been that Frank's questions were thoughtful but not intrusive, but it might have had something to do with her growing awareness that, whether he knew it or not, this reporter was kinky. More than that, he had a submissive streak.

Miss Juliet crossed her legs again, and looked down at her own toes, the nails painted warm gold. Out of the corner of her eye, she checked Frank's response; he was looking at her feet as well.

"Oliver loved my feet," she said. The reporter made a little muffled sound, not quite a word. "He liked to kiss my toes," Juliet went on, and wiggled them. Frank said nothing, so Juliet stood up, and smiled at him. "Would you like a glass of wine? I'm going to have one."

He put down his notebook. "Uh, yes. Yes, please. Thank you."

When she came back into the room, with a bottle of white Burgundy and two glasses, she could tell he was unsure of how to proceed. She decided not to make it too easy for him.

She filled the glasses, handed him one and sat back down, crossing her legs at the ankle.

"What made you pick this type of journalism?" she asked. Frank stared at her, evidently startled. She didn't relent.

"Did you start at your local paper, or was it music reviews, or fanzines?"

"Um, it was news," he said. "But, you know, I didn't want to be shitty to people. There was too much stuff where we were supposed to have made our minds up about them before the interview. I thought—I think—people should be able to put their side of a story. Whatever it is."

Miss Juliet finished her tea and glanced at the kitchen clock. Past midday, so having a glass of wine would not be unreasonable. Nor, she decided, would it be unreasonable to grant Frank's request. He didn't approach her for an interview that often and never seemed to take offence on the occasions she refused. She had not often been burned by a journalist, though she had seen it happen to people she knew. In the years since their initial encounter, she had occasionally discussed such clusterfucks with Frank, whether that had involved condemnation of the manipulative interviewer, or exasperation with the naïve but publicity-hungry interviewee, both of them had been in broad agreement about red flags and mistakes to avoid.

"Shagging your interviewees is usually a bad idea," he had once said, and Juliet had agreed, at least to the extent that shagging your interviewer is not recommended.

Of course, they hadn't shagged. They hadn't fucked, or even touched each other's genitals, not on their first encounter, nor at any time after. But, after a long conversation, that hot spring afternoon, Frank had knelt on the floor, at her feet, and he had lifted each foot in turn to his lips, and she had stroked his hair and told him that she understood his desires, and could teach him to understand them, and he had come in his pants. She had been prepared, at the time, for his article to be a vicious hit piece, despite his gratitude and contentment when he left her flat. It hadn't been, and this had made them, to an extent, friends.

Glass of wine in hand, she went back to the office, re-opened the email and composed her reply.

Oh go on then. But stop calling me Twinkletoes, or else.

FAT SLUT

Allison Armstrong

My first thought is that this isn't going to work.

Okay, let me back up.

My first thought is, *I can't believe we're doing this.*

I can't believe *I'm* doing this.

I can't believe I'm doing this with *Emily*, my BBW Porn Mom, occasional costar, longtime crush, and longer time friend.

I glance at them out of the corner of my eye. They're wearing leggings, their signature leopard print clinging to their gorgeous legs, with bright high heels and a cowl-neck sweater that flops off one shoulder, displaying the lilies that crown their sleeve tattoo. Their two-tone hair is pulled back in a casual pony tail, but they've gone to the trouble of false eyelashes and fuchsia lipstick and, when they take a sip of their bubble tea, I see that their nub-short nails are painted to match. In my Riot Don't Diet t-shirt, stretch-denim skirt, and canvas sneakers, I'm nowhere *near* as put-together. I imagine I look like the inept baby sibling getting shown the ropes of bra shopping and sex appeal by a more experienced, older femme.

Which is *hot*.

But I also feel like I didn't try hard enough.

Not that I'm planning to stay dressed.

It crosses my mind, again, that I'm about to have *very* public sex in the only real plus-size lingerie store around. This is where I buy my work clothes. The quarter-cup bras that will support my F-cups, the jewel-toned negligees that show up best on camera, the under-bust corsets made for actual fat people. Not to mention the slip shorts that help me avoid chub rub when I'm not filming.

And *that's* when I think, *This isn't going to work.*

I stop in my tracks outside an electronics store.

"I'm not sure I can do this," I confess.

At work, Emily's whole brand is "Tiger Milf", at least it has been since the laugh lines around their eyes got visible enough that they couldn't hide them with concealer and good lighting anymore. But they've always bossed me around, even back when we first met, and they've *always* been good at it. So when I tell them I'm not sure about this whole scene after all, part of me is hoping that they'll bully me into doing it anyway.

It's not like we've never done scenes together—after they moved back to town, we first ran into each other at a play party off twelfth—but mostly our shared sex life is "professional collaborators" not "friends with benefits". This is new territory. And I want *so badly* to shift into that territory. I want sleepovers when the cameras are off. I want waffle brunch together, at home, when we have keys to each others' apartments. I want them to kiss me in public.

132

And suddenly I'm scared.

When I told them—three weeks earlier when we were both Not Smoking on a friend's balcony—that I fantasize about being fucked in a lingerie fitting room, I'd mostly said it to get their attention.

They'd broken up with Kaiden—who'd turned out to be a typical white boy—just after New Year's, and our conversation had been threatening to turn back to what an asshole-slash-sweetheart he'd been. Which was the last thing I'd wanted. Looking at Emily, at the way the balcony string lights lit their face softly and made the fuchsia streaks in their dark hair light up, the way their winged eyeliner was smudged after a night of laughter, not to mention the way the plunging neckline of their leopard print top stunningly displayed their internet-famous cleavage, I'd decided that distracting them with my willingness to be a total slut was *one hundred percent* the right thing to do.

"Really?" they'd asked, straightening up, more interested than I'd expected.

"Sure," I'd faltered. "I mean, the whole point of lingerie is to feel sexy—"

"I want details!" they'd announced and, to my surprise, I was able to oblige.

My fantasy had always been this vague impression of velvet drapes and discarded lacy things, plus the ever-present possibility of being caught. But the more Emily pressed me for details, their eyes taking on an excited gleam, the more my fantasy took form.

"Holy shit, Parul..." they'd breathed, shaking their head, when I'd finished. Then, "Um. I'm gonna head back inside."

I was so sure I'd put them off that I'd stayed on the balcony for ages. When I finally went back in, Emily was on the couch with their heels off and their feet in the lap of some butch I didn't know. Maybe it's not surprising that I hadn't expected them to run with it. I definitely hadn't expected them to text me, two weeks after, telling me everything was ready and to clear my calendar and do whatever personal topiary I needed to do to feel good getting fucked in a fitting room while most likely wearing at least one article of lingerie that I hadn't paid for.

"You can pay for it after," they'd told me, at brunch, looking at me over the rim of their coffee cup. "It'll be fine."

But now that we're actually here... what if it's *not* fine? What if the staff person is weirdly keen to make a sale? What if there's a sudden lingerie rush at 2pm on a Tuesday afternoon? What if we get there, and everything is perfect... right up until I take my clothes off and Emily sees me under the awful florescent tube lighting, instead of the carefully positioned soft box and ring light that we usually work with? What if they're only doing this as a favour and my "bad fatty" body, that's *never* going to look like Bishamber Das or Liris Crosse, turns them off?

What if they only want me when they're acting?

Emily looks at me for a long moment.

"We don't have to," they say quietly. They're looking at me like they want to let me off the hook, but are disappointed about it.

"You're not mad, are you?"

"What? No!" They chew their lip, swallow hard enough for me to notice it, then shrug lightly. "I was just, y'know, looking forward to this."

I blink.

"You—" I can feel myself blushing, which, this early in spring, is definitely going to show. The flush creeps up my neck, heating my ears, and I can't help it. I grin. "You were looking forward to it?"

They look at me like I have two heads, then lean in close.

"Did you not notice?" they ask, lowering their voice even further. "The way you had me squirming at that party? I had to go to the bathroom and get myself off!"

My mouth falls *right* open at that revelation.

"Are you serious?" I ask. Suddenly the day's plan isn't looking like nearly such a terrible idea.

"I'm *so* serious," they answer. "Look," they go on, gesturing with their bubble tea. "Like I said. You don't have to. If you're uncomfortable, or you think it's too risky, we can always do something else. I mean," they add, "I did kind of just confessed that I totally want to bone you. So, like... if you're into it, we could just go to my place. I could make you try on *my* clothes."

Oh my god...

I try so hard not to squeal, but Emily just said they *totally want to bone me*! The announcement has caused a certain part of my anatomy to start gushing like a faucet.

"Um," I say, trying to contain my glee. "Okay, listen. A lot of that was literally just 'what if you're not into it' stuff. So. I'm definitely feeling a lot better about this—" They look so relieved at that, I want to hug them. "But," I continue, "some of it's just... are you *sure* that we're not going to end up getting banned from the *mall*—god, how is this even my life?—for..." I gesticulate, waving my hands, trying to find the right word, "...Reasons?"

Emily giggles.

"Gosh," they say, "I can't imagine what you mean by 'reasons'." They take another sip of their bubble tea, before continuing, "So, obviously I can't guarantee that... Reasons... won't happen," they say. "Or, I mean... You know what I mean. I can't guarantee that this is a risk-free endeavour. We might have to bail, if there are too many people. But Jaz—you remember, Jaz, you met them at that poetry thing—they're working today, and they swear Tuesdays are always quiet."

They bump my shoulder with their own. "But I thought that was part of the *thrill*. I thought you *wanted* to imagine some unsuspecting straight lady, looking at beige basics on a late lunch, to hear you getting fucked like the filthy queer you are."

I splutter. My cunt is already drooling. At this rate I'm going to soak through my panties before we even hit the fitting room.

"You're not wrong," I admit.

"So let's go," Emily says, and starts walking again, leading me on towards the unsuspecting satin and lace-trimmed den of iniquity. I follow, eagerly, behind, watching Emily's juicy ass all the way there.

Really, the shop is just a standard mall store. It has non-full-spectrum neon lights, walls of bras and poly-satin robes, and a back fitting area with several cubicles that you get to through a burgundy velvet curtain. The only thing that makes it stand out is that its size range goes up to a 5XL and the buyers aren't so hard of thinking that they assume all fat people would want from underwear is a way to make themselves look skinnier by whatever means necessary.

"Ready?" Emily asks, dropping their empty bubble tea cup into a nearby bin.

"As I'll ever be."

The person behind the cash desk—I guess that's Jaz—is unfolding shiny black something-or-others and hanging them on hangers. They look stupendously bored, but glance in our direction and swap knowing nods with Emily when we walk into the otherwise empty store.

Emily doesn't waste any time. Their hand on the small of my back, they steer me towards the sale racks, where the clerk is most likely to keep ignoring us. As soon as there's a display of cheap panties between us and the cash desk, they stop me and press their tits against my back, running one hand proprietorially over my ass.

"Get in that fitting room and strip," they murmur, giving my ass a squeeze. "I'm going to decide what you'll be wearing for me today."

They give me a little push towards the velvet-draped cubicles, and I do as I'm told.

The fitting area is familiar—like I said, I buy my work clothes here—and the burgundy ultrasuede ottoman is right where I'm expecting it to be. I choose a cubicle at the very back of the fitting area, slide the curtains shut and sit down to unlace my shoes. I unzip my skirt and wiggle out of it, peel off my panties, tuck my socks into my sneakers and brush the lint off my toes. I can't help feeling the familiar buzz of excitement as I strip off my t-shirt and drop my bra.

I'm about to have sex in public! I think, as I flip my shirt inside out and lay it across the ottoman.

It's funny. I'm so completely okay with roping an entire store—even an empty one—into being part of my power fantasy, my public sex game, but I'd hate to think I was being a jerk by making a mess of the furniture. I perch on top of my t-shirt, and run my hands over my body, feeling the nerves wake up. This is like any collaboration, any scene at a party. I take a moment to squeeze my kegel muscles, take some deep breaths, play with my nipples and pull my own hair.

Yeah.

I feel my turn-on heating up, just as I hear Emily's voice floating towards me.

"I've got some stuff you might like," they call from the other end of the fitting area. Then, much closer, so close I can see their feet under the hem of the curtain, "Open up and let's see what we've got."

I slide the velvet drapes back and put myself on display. It's hard not to slip into work mode, remind myself to point my toes, lift my tits, pull my shoulders back. It's hard not to fondle my body under their gaze. But I don't want to be Naughty Pema, my alter ego, right now. Right now I'm just Parul, awkwardly naked in front of my unexpectedly-mutual crush.

Emily has their arms full of shiny fabric. Mostly negligees and robes, by the looks of things. They dump them unceremoniously on the floor.

"Hang those up," they order, quietly, gesturing at the row of tiny hooks in the cubicle wall.

I move to pull the curtain closed again, but—

"No, no," Emily chides. "Keep those open. You know," they add, pulling up the one 'husband chair' in the whole room. "Like your legs."

I feel the hot rush of shame and, on its heels, the equally hot throb of arousal. I nod my head and start matching bras to garter belts. It's not hard to notice that there's only one set of panties in the whole collection. A high-waist pair of deep violet velvet briefs, more mesh and ribbon than anything else, the split gusset an invitation in and of itself. I almost want to buy them, just for work. But I can guess why they're here, and I hang them, with their matching balconet bra, carefully towards the end of the rack.

"Try on the blue one first," Emily says, gesturing at a sapphire satin negligee near the front of the rack. I pull it on over my head, shimmying into it, then scooping my breasts into the structured cups before reaching around to fasten the hook-and-eye at the back.

"Turn around," says Emily, and I offer a little twirl. They grin.

"One more time," they say. "Slowly."

I give them my best three-point turn.

"It's cute," Emily concedes. "Put it in the 'maybe' pile." They start to rummage in their purse. "Try the green one now."

The green one in question is a sheer, emerald babydoll, split open from sternum to hem. The flimsy fabric floats over my ass like nothing. There's enough structure in the underwire to give me some support but the cups are stretchy and I can see my nipples, tight and erect, right through them, as entirely on display as my thick thighs and the swell of my belly. I can feel the air against my bare skin where the mesh parts expose me.

"Come here," Emily says, beckoning to me. While I was changing clothes, they were finding a black latex glove and stretching it into place over their hand.

Oh.

I'm suddenly self-conscious, uncomfortable at the thought of stepping out of the cubicle, even though anyone who came into the fitting area would be able to see *everything* already.

"I said come here," Emily reminds me.

I make myself step out of the cubicle, fidgeting with my hem, trying to hide behind my own arms. I watch them check over their shoulder.

"All the way," they say. "Come stand beside me."

My breath goes shallow, but I step into position. I'm expecting them to touch me. To fondle my tits with their gloved hand, to squeeze them or tease my nipples through the delicate mesh. I'm not expecting them to suck my nipple into their mouth, sheer fabric and all.

I gasp, gripping their shoulder, and try to swallow the whimper that, despite my best efforts, manages to escape me. They lap and suck my nipple through the thin fabric, and I grit my teeth, squeeze my eyes shut, take tiny, shallow sips of air, and try not to groan. Their mouth feels so good. Hot and wet, their tongue firm as it strokes and circles. I can feel my wetness starting to ooze down my thigh.

"You like that, don't you?" Emily asks, relenting, letting my swollen nipple go.

I nod, catching my breath. I look down, and there's an obvious, darker spot on the fabric where their saliva has soaked through.

They trail their fingers down my sternum, and I shiver.

"Good," they murmur. They brush the thin mesh aside, slide their hand down my ribs, over my flushed skin, pausing at my hip. I can feel the heat of their hand through the latex of their glove.

"Spread your legs," they tell me, barely above a whisper.

I shuffle my feet apart, all too aware of my burning ears, my bare ass and sopping cunt.

They slide their hand deftly between my legs, cupping my cunt in their palm.

"You're really enjoying this," they comment, tickling my labia with their fingers, slicking them in my come.

"I am," I admit.

I'm turned on, that's undeniable. But I want to drop. I want to sink into that space where I'm all focused eagerness to please and I feel like I can take anything. Take *everything*. They slide one finger, too easily, into my cunt, and I groan, a little surprised, a *lot* aroused.

Yes, I think. *Use me. Make me hot for it.*

Instead, they remove their finger from my too-hungry, disappointed cunt.

"Mm. Eager," Emily muses to themself. "I think you're just about ready." They shift their attention to my face. "Go put on the purple ones."

My cunt clenches, just a little, and my stomach flutters, as I step back into the cubical. There must be a dozen things still hanging on the hooks, but I strip off the babydoll and retrieve the deep violet panties from their place on the end. I slip them on and slide them up my legs. The mesh fabric hugs my ass, the strips of velvet ribbon pressing in just enough to make it seem like my own panties are copping a feel. The matching bra is an afterthought. Until I put it on. Plush velvet cups my tits, just barely enough to support them, my nipples obvious through the sheer mesh that makes up most of the balconet. I stroke the fabric, admire myself in the mirror, slide my hands reverently over my skin. My wet cunt is soaking the panties, but even if it wasn't, I know I'd be taking them home.

Is it terrible that I'm distracting myself so well I don't notice them come up behind me?

"I knew you'd like them," Emily says, wrapping their arms around me.

They slide their hands over my breasts, dip their fingers into the bra, palming my tits, and I feel my nipples harden under their hands. Slowly, they push their knee between my thighs, spreading my legs again.

"Look at how wet you are," they comment. "Making a mess of my favourite leggings."

They pinch one of my nipples between latex-smoothed fingers, pull their other hand out of my bra to twist their bare fingers in my hair. They press their knuckles against my scalp, my hair gripped firmly in their fist, and ease my head back 'til I can feel their breath on my earlobe.

"You're a filthy slut who wants to get fucked aren't you," they murmur against my ear. "That greedy cunt wants to swallow my fist, isn't that right?" They give me a little shake, and I gasp. "I'm sure I just asked you a question," they go on, pulling gently at my nipple. "Did I ask you a question?"

"You did," I gasp. They tug my nipple and the sensation goes straight to my clit, lighting it up.

"And?" they press.

"Yes," I pant. My cunt is molten between my slippery thighs. "Yes, I'm a filthy slut who wants to get fucked."

I feel the curve of their mouth, against my earlobe, as they smile.

"You'll have to give me a *very* good show," they tell me, releasing my nipple. They slide their other hand out of my bra, and wrap it around my throat. The latex is smooth, all silk and grip against my skin. Just the barest pressure against my larynx, and—

Oh.

Yes.

I feel my shoulders drop.

I feel my *everything* drop.

"Show me that ass," Emily murmurs and, without even thinking, I bend at the hips for them, rest my hands on my knees, spread my legs just a little farther.

Yes.

"Very good," they tell me.

Keeping their bare hand on the back of my neck, they let go of my throat, move their other hand downward. When I feel the latex of their glove part the split gusset of my panties, I whimper. They press their palm more firmly to my cunt and I feel the squish and squelch of my wetness.

"Who's an excellent slut," Emily croons, keeping their voice low as their hand slips and slides between my legs. I can feel my clit swelling against the velvet. "Who's an unprofessional whore," they go on, their voice turning cruel, "Putting in volunteer hours and undercutting their union?"

Emily slaps my cunt hard enough to sting—hard enough to make me gasp—then goes back to rubbing me, sliding their fingers over the hard nub of my clit, making me whimper and mewl and bite my lip to keep quiet. I feel them spread my labia, and the shock of their fingers—at a guess, more than two—pushing into me makes me moan much louder than I meant to.

"I bet you yowl like a cat when you come," they comment.

I *mean...*

But their fingers are curling in my cunt, and their thumb is sliding against my swollen clit, electric pleasure thrilling through me, making me shiver, making me shudder, my hands braced against my knees, which are threatening to buckle.

All I can do is pant and gasp and try to prove them wrong.

It doesn't work. I whimper as they find the rhythm they've used a hundred times to make me come. But there's no camera this time, no phone mount for close-ups, only their fingers working my cunt, only years of their knowing exactly how to make me do what they want.

I groan as their hand on the back of my neck shifts, fisting in my hair. They drag my head up, forcing me to look directly into the fitting room mirror.

"Look at that fat slut," Emily orders, their hand moving between my thighs, their thumb sliding across my clit, the pressure in my cunt building hard. "Look at that fat brown bombshell who loves to get fucked just right."

I look.

My shaking thighs and pendulous round belly. My thick arms. My breasts spilling out of the bra, jiggling as I pant and gasp. My full lips, parting. My dark hair gripped in Emily's fist. They make me come like that.

Looking at my round, brown body, the way my mouth strains open, the way my belly rolls and my hips flex as my cunt clenches around their fingers and my orgasm rips through me.

"Aren't you gorgeous," Emily breathes. "You gorgeous, perfect, filthy, fat slut."

They aren't wrong.

My cunt grips their fingers again, as they curl against my g-spot, helping me finish. They drag their fingers slowly out of my cunt, slap my labia again, then slide their hand out from between my shaking legs. I can see the long ropes of jizz drooling from my cunt, clinging to my thighs, staining the purple velvet dark, and I smile.

When I've caught my breath, Emily helps me straighten up. I laugh, easing the stiffness out of my knees, realizing that we got away with it, that I got exactly what I wanted.

"You did good," Emily tells me, peeling off their glove. "I'm proud of you."

I rip the tag off the panties, wondering if I can get away with just walking out in them. Emily passes me my skirt, and I shimmy into it. I'm wearing these panties home either way.

"What do you want to do next?" Emily asks. I'm surprised to hear them sound shy.

I smile, yanking the tag of my new, velvet bra.

"Didn't you say something about going to your place?" I ask, flushed with victory and ready for round two.

"I did," Emily admits, grinning as they watch me shrug my t-shirt on.

They lean in, cup my chin, and kiss me like an invitation.

"Come on," they say, taking my hand. "Let's go."

PATRIOT

Ralph Greco, Jr.

"You'll do it?" the President asked, looking up at me from under his peppered bangs.

"Considering," I said, bringing the toe of my left stiletto to his mouth.

"We go back a long way, De," he said, after kissing it." I could only ever ask this of you."

"I know."

"It is a serious proposition," he continued, after another soft kiss, as I brought my other patent-leather toe down on his naked inner thigh.

Arnold inhaled and spread his legs even wider as my foot traced a deep furrow to his hard penis.

"Oh, it hurts," he moaned, lips still puckering round my heel, lying back even further.

I knew how much this man could take: this was only the start of his limit, but the President and I needed to talk, get beyond this session, if I was even to consider the bombshell he had just dropped in my naked lap. Through my years of service in the O.O., I had run roughshod over many of this handsome man's more-than-odd requests, but what he had been telling me these past ten minutes was a whopper!

"Go ahead..." I said, looking down hard at him, but smiling. "Get it over with."

The President began masturbating as I mused:
The little girl who would be king.

It only took me a few hours the next morning to pack. Arnold had already left, so I didn't need my usual latex, and other than the small martinet I always kept locked to my belt loop, I wouldn't pack any instruments or toys.

While home, I had the chance to call Dawn. I was wondering if she had been picked by the Prime Minister she was working for. For some reason I still couldn't quite surmise, the European leaders always liked to have more than one dominatrix attending their needs. At the same time, their American counterparts usually only enjoyed the attentions of one (sure, there were stories about President Taft, but nothing ever confirmed). I knew Dawn well: she had such exquisite expertise with enemas that I'm sure she was one of the favorites, if not the greatest one, of the old man she served.

"Ironic," Dawn said, after we had passed a quick hello. "That's what it is. I-fucking-ronic!"

"We go through our days aching to find new ways to get them to submit, and they are the ones who think of this?" I said. "But, shit, girl, I can't run the place!"

"Me neither," Dawn agreed, "but we really won't be, anyway."

"Look," I continued, "I'll call you from there. Let me get settled then, well...shit, I'm sure we're gonna have lots to talk about the next couple of weeks."

That night I was walking through security at The House. I was a frequent visitor, and no act of aggression had occurred in the Capitol City since before the Civil War. Still, the relaxed security was considered a polite nod to traditionalism; as ever: men needed to at least, hold their guns.

A girl like me is born and bred for this life. My mother was a dominatrix before me, as were her two sisters. Fancy cars, quiet dinners, laughing on the arm of a man of distinction, partying in a stuffy crowd while managing a knowing nod across a room, which indicates to that same man that in just a few short hours, he will be across my lap, pleading for me not to spank him, even though he longs for me to do so. This was my life and had been the same for those women I most respected. I had no idea what other women did with their time, or what they thought of women like me. As far back as anyone alive could remember, we were seen as just part of things, a worldwide sorority that went with the limos and dinner parties. But there were times like this, when I actually stopped long enough to think about where I was (right then, standing in the doorway of the lavender and blue bedroom on the second floor) that I almost felt sorry for all those other women who weren't in service... And maybe a little sorry for myself, that I would never know the quiet of their lives, as well.

Handry Greenstan found me an hour later. I was sitting in The Blue Room, sipping a scotch and soda, when the petite First Lady entered, smiled, and sat right down next to me.

"It's quiet with him gone," she offered, her deep green eyes staring straight at me.

149

The First Lady and I had been on a friendly basis for a good twelve years, but this was the first time we would be sitting down for a chat. I thought it best to be as hospitable as possible.

This was *her* house, after all.

"Can I get you a drink?" I asked, scooting forward on the comfortable leather couch.

"No, I..." she started as I stood.

"I'm gonna refresh mine," I said, to put her at her ease. "Let me get you something."

"Okay..." Handry said, looking down once and then back at me. "...whatever you're having."

"Doesn't look all that with-it, does he?" the First Lady said when I turned back from the mini-bar.

With the two full glasses in hand, I walked over to the handsome lady. Handry had her green-eyed gaze fixed hard on President Grant's portrait over the couch. Her thin lips were spread in a kind smile as I handed her her glass and sat once again.

"Maybe the portrait doesn't do him justice," I tried, wiggling into my still-warm spot.

"Freaking walrus," she said, tipping her drink up to the portrait.

I had to sip my drink for fear I'd spill it as I chuckled with her.

"Well, none of them are much without a good woman behind them," I said, lifting my glass in quick salute to the lady sitting next to me.

The First Lady looked down from Grant to me.

"You mean, without the women who *beat* them."

"No, with all due respect," I lightly disagreed as Handry sipped her drink, "I meant what I said. You are his strength. You provide the fuel that he runs on."

"Funny, I've often thought the same of you," she admitted after a quick sip.

I had been lucky with Handry all these years. Most of the girls are merely tolerated, a part of political life that was once private policy but had been passed into law the past century. Although she was well aware of it, it was up to me, now, to reassure this comely, pretty woman that I simply provided a service.

This would be my first real act of diplomacy.

"I can do what I do because of what you've built with the President," I started. "Even Mrs. Grant admitted her limitations: First Ladies have enough to do."

"You don't know the half of it," she said, chuckling again, and lifted her glass to clink mine.

"I see the marks..." she admitted, after a long gulp of the amber liquid. "...and I know he does deserve them."

"That's what I try to tell him," I said, and we laughed again, clinked our glasses again, and took another simultaneous sip.

This was going to be an all-night drunk.

"Is it hard for other women in your field?" she asked. "I mean, the ones without steady clients."

"Used to be," I said. "But there has been such a steady network since the second Euro accord, it's not all that hard for any of us now. But working this high up is an exception. And, assuredly, one I'm grateful for."

"You do your job well, De," the First Lady assured me.

"Thanks," I said, and we both sipped again.

"What do you think about these two weeks?" Handry asked, after a full minute of silence.

"I am confused by it, actually," I began, "God knows, I know many ways to break a man's will; things to say, things to do... And instruments to do it with. But I have to tell you, having these men leave their doms in charge for two weeks is such a subtle and perverse humiliation that I'm really jealous I hadn't thought of it myself."

Handry and I laughed a good minute over that one. When we settled down, and had a few more sips, she looked to the corner of the room, the one directly opposite the mini-bar, and her eyes settled on Mrs. Grant's ancient riding crop.

"How could she have known?" the First Lady mused out loud.

"My guess is that they both reasoned it out together," I offered. "You don't just come out to the President and say, 'I think you need to strip naked and get on all fours tonight. I have the urge to beat your ass. I know it will make you a better leader.'"

"Amazing," she said, still staring at the crop.

"What always interested me most..." I continued, "...was how every government fell into line. I mean, by any objective standards, at the time, we were a relatively young nation. They could have all thrown us out as pariahs. Imagine our status then?"

"They would have been hypocrites when we all know almost every other seat of power had a woman making that seat red."

"Well said," I smiled, and again we clinked.

"Are you a student of history?" the First Lady asked, after another sip.

152

"Maybe more so than most," I countered. "Seeing as where I ply my wares? But…" and this is where my diplomacy was going to be put to the test, I knew, "…I am merely his mistress. A good one for sure." I added a smile. "Maybe even the best. But your husband doesn't want anyone for his lover other than you."

Handry smiled, sipped, and sat back in the couch, obviously relieved we were speaking so plainly, enjoying the warmth of the drink, and my diplomacy.

I slept like a baby that night. I had always imagined a constantly-humming machine turning under the deepest bowels of The White House. The thought that I was this motor's keeper for two weeks should have grown a deep insomnia. The pulse of this place: the import of the musty summer Washington DC nights; the comings and goings at all hours; the press always at the door; the phone calls, emails, and other insidious secret communiques. I imagined I would have to do a lot of heavy drinking, just to numb the constant chatter. But, to my surprise, I wasn't the least bit bothered to be sleeping here.

Or being President.

Arnold had assured me I could do the job, and I had no fear that I couldn't. The President is a well-respected man, as are all the other leaders of the world, but I knew these men were so well insulated by aides and advisers that The White House and the seats of other governments practically ran themselves; that old motor I imagined probably ran on solar power, as every other homeowner's did nowadays. Pretty much what Dawn had implied. Whoever said that the office made the man was as far off the mark as you can get. The

153

man made the office. The White House of Arnold Greenstan's administration worked as smoothly and as calmly as the lanky man with the rather thick cock moved.

I took my morning coffee out onto the terrace of my bedroom, which faced a glorious rose garden on the east side of the house. I let the ten-o'clock heat envelope my long, bare legs. It was going to be another scorcher; probably hotter than the ninety-five degrees we had had the day before. I was blessing the air conditioning I could feel tickling me through the open bedroom door when I heard light footsteps on the stone floor behind me.

"Yes?" I asked, turning to the tall, lean man known as Brill.

He had been the President's aide since the days of Arnold's first term, and yet he hadn't spoken but a sentence or two to me in all my years with his boss. I didn't particularly like the way he always seemed to be regarding me from under his heavy brown bangs or always slightly bending away from me whenever I made my way past him. Still, he was fiercely loyal to Arnold.

"There is a phone call," he said, and I watched his eyes regard me with, as always, a slight mocking cast to his blue-gray irises. This time though, I spied his gaze quickly run to my chest, and I realized then that my light robe was open enough to show quite an ample amount of my high bosom.

'If you were mine, I'd swat you ten quick ones for that look,' I thought to myself and tried desperately to keep the blush from my cheeks.

"Will you take it here?" the man continued, and I snapped out of my fantasy.

154

"Ye...Yes, please," I said, turning fully in the chair now. I let the robe fall open nearly all the way, but Brill ignored me, turned, and walked back into my room. Seconds later, he appeared before me again, a portable gray phone in his hand.

"Thanks," I said as the man handed me the phone, then left the terrace.

As I had assumed, it was Dawn.

"You don't answer your cell?"

"You know the nightly scramble and block? I didn't get to log in yet this morning."

"Well, the caca hit the A.C. while you were asleep. They fucking ran one on us."

Dawn was talking loudly to battle the transcontinental lines: we may have had the world unified in peaceful accord, but even with the lift on advertising, National Eurocom still had mighty problems with their satellites. Her voice sounded piqued beyond the usual volume and pitch she had to manage when calling me.

"What's the matter?"

"Goddamn them, De," she said, a hint of a chuckle in her throat. It was as if she was put off yet tickled, all at the same time.

"Dawn, what are you talking about?" I asked, a slight feeling of dread creeping up my spine.

I knew my friend well. There was no way she would have called the house, and ambled through explaining who she was, to get to me this morning, if this wasn't an important call. With her own man gone, she'd have to have better things to do with her day, I knew.

"You haven't heard," she said, not asking. "You haven't heard a thing."

155

"Dawn, I just got up for Christ's sake," I said.

"Well, I hope you're sitting down," she said and then continued with words I had hoped I would never be hearing, but somehow knew I would: "They ran on us. Your President, my Prime Minister, Manny and Diane's Czar, all the others. They ran one on us, and they ain't coming back."

"What?" I asked, jumping up to the cool tile floor. "What the hell are you saying?"

"Check it out," my sister said, allowing a loud giggle to escape. "Go ahead. Call me back when you get your shit together. I mean, I can't handle this, De. I really can't."

"I'll call you back," I said once again, marveling at both Dawn's panic yet her good humor.

Like me, I assumed she was too shocked to really consider what the hell was happening.

I ran into the thick-draped bedroom, out of my open bedroom door, and through to the hallway beyond. To my surprise, I ran smack into Brill. He was smiling a thin-lipped grin I had yet to see him manage for me.

"The President believed it would be best for you to find out through your own channels."

"This has got to be a joke."

"No." Brill said, "If you will follow me back into your bedroom."

I did and he said: "Please," pointing softly at the bed. I sat as demurely as possible; no open-robe teasing.

"As you are well aware, the President and his contemporaries began this mission in earnest," Brill began.

156

"I know what it was for," I said. "Come on, Brill, lighten up; we both know what I do. Hell, the entire country knows what I do."

"Then you will be well aware of the lasting effects, shall we say, of this latest wrinkle to the plan."

"This is more than just a wrinkle, buddy," I spat, sitting bolt upright. "The President has to come back!"

"I'm afraid he won't," Brill said. "At least not for a long time. He and the others have formulated this, Ultimate Humiliation, as he called it, to last indefinitely."

"But I can't *last indefinitely*," I nearly screamed. "Brill, I can't be President!"

The man smiled again, then turned to leave.

"Brill," I said, stood up, and ran to him. I grabbed his arm and pulled as hard as I could to turn the tall guy around. I realized right then he sported a very sinewy set of muscles under his expensive suit jacket.

"I can't be President," I repeated, softly this time. The last thing I wanted was to hear myself really say that out loud.

"If the skills and strengths I have heard you possess are any clues to your abilities, then I have no doubt you can run this office. Besides...." the man said, and for the second time in my life, smiled at me. "...I truly believe the world will be a better place if you, and the women like you, are in charge."

Careful what you wish for, they say, though how could I ever have wished for this? I know all about wishing, needing, wanting. I provide my service to quell hunger, quench thirsts, and answer prayers. This government and all the others in the world are built on exploring hidden desires, twisting the regular everyday grind of being a leader into the nighttime play of being a dog, slave, and follower. But the followers, the dogs, the little boys, have had the last laugh.

Indeed, the submissive in any relationship is actually the dominant. He or she sets the limits, he or she provides the clues, allows the specifics, acquiesces control. President Arnold and all those other leaders set the limits here; they allowed the plan, their mistresses (me included) merely facilitated their wants.

I thought I knew Arnold Greenstan. I thought that after you have a man at your heels, a six-inch dildo shoved up his ass, and a clothespin pinching his scrotum, you know that man well. But, as President Grant said, "the higher a man rises, the more often he should be checked for his desires."

It was check and mate for all of us, now.

CPSIA information can be obtained
at www.ICGtesting.com
Printed in the USA
BVHW081059291121
622764BV00003B/291

9 781948 780315